"As tragedy upon tragedy befalls the sweet but naive Leira in this Bronze Age–set tale, readers will cheer for her to succeed, grow, and to find her way in this new world...An eye-opening look at how difficult it is when one's status changes in life, and how attitude can shape outcome. Beautiful writing and a fast-moving plot will give young historical fiction fans much to love."
—*School Library Journal* ★ **Starred Review**

"Wendy Orr has crafted a sympathetic, memorable heroine whose struggles and challenges transcend time from the Bronze Age to modern day.... While suitable for middle grade students and a wonderful introduction to mythology and discussions surrounding puberty, spirituality, class, mental health, death and disaster, *Swallow's Dance* is one of those rare books that is also just a great story, an epic tale for all ages. **Highly Recommended."**
—*CM Magazine*

"Top notch historical fiction for those who like it ancient!...The scenes of devastation – earthquake in Santorini, tsunami in Crete – are riveting to experience through the lens of a survivor."—*Youth Services Book Review*

Praise for *Dragonfly Song* by Wendy Orr

★ Finalist for the Rocky Mountain Book Award
★ Finalist for the TD Canadian Children's Literature Award
★ Finalist for the Sunburst Award
★ Finalist for the Maine Student Book Award
★ Junior Library Guild selection
★ Bank Street Best Book

"Orr tells her tale in both narrative poetry and prose for an effect that is both fanciful and urgent, drawing a rich fantasy landscape filled with people and creatures worthy of knowing. An introductory note describes Orr's inspiration in the legend of the Minotaur, but her story is no retelling but a meditation on rejection and acceptance, on determination and self-determination….As mesmerizing as a mermaid's kiss, the story dances with emotion, fire, and promise." —*Kirkus* ★ Starred Review

"The Bronze Age setting makes for a unique backdrop, and Aissa is a sympathetic character. Her struggles are heartrending, and made more so by the lyrical storytelling style. The descriptions of the dances are especially vivid. Hand-sell this unusual tale to fans of Shannon Hale's historical fantasies." —*School Library Journal*

"Orr tells Aissa's tale in a lyrical mix of narrative poetry and prose, using lush, vivid language to create an unparalleled fantasy world full of life and lively characters. While young readers with a special interest in history will immediately be drawn into this meticulously researched, literary story, its fast-paced, adventurous, epic feel will undoubtedly appeal to all readers." —*Booklist*

"Loosely inspired by the story of the Minotaur, this is a thoughtful reimagining of the rituals involved in Bronze Age worship and belief, with the plot taking several fascinating turns that showcase the various vocations involved in village life....An unusually thoughtful offering in the middle-school mythology genre." —*Bulletin of the Center for Children's Books*

"*Dragonfly Song* is an impressive work of middle-grade historical fiction. Aissa is a brave, tenacious girl, who rebels against the constraints of her life without appearing anachronistic. There isn't a lot of young people's fiction set in the Bronze Age, and the details here are lovingly researched, creating a transportive world. Especially noteworthy is the representation of religion in a pre-Christian setting, as the book explores both its beauty and brutality." —*Quill & Quire*

"A work of beauty. From the stunning cover to the mythological imagery and lyrical prose, readers are drawn in and carried along on an intense ride....*Dragonfly Song* would make a perfect read-aloud chapter book for middle grade teachers. While the academic cross curricular subject areas are obvious, including history, mythology, religion, spirituality, even bullying, I enjoyed this story simply as a pleasure read. **Highly Recommended.**" —*CM Magazine*

CUCKOO'S FLIGHT

FLIGHT

WENDY ORR

pajamapress

First published in Canada and the United States in 2021

Text copyright © 2021 Wendy Orr

This edition copyright © 2021 Pajama Press Inc.

Published simultaneously with Allen & Unwin: Crow's Nest, New South Wales, Australia, 2021

10 9 8 7 6 5 4 3 2 1

www.pajamapress.ca   info@pajamapress.ca

The publisher gratefully acknowledges the support of the Canada Council for the Arts and the Ontario Arts Council for its publishing program. We acknowledge the financial support of the Government of Canada through the Canada Book Fund (CBF) for our publishing activities.

Library and Archives Canada Cataloguing in Publication

Title: Cuckoo's flight / Wendy Orr.
Names: Orr, Wendy, 1953- author.
Identifiers: Canadiana 20200361961 | ISBN 9781772781908 (hardcover)
Classification: LCC PS8577.R77 C83 2021 | DDC jC813/.54—dc23

Publisher Cataloging-in-Publication Data (U.S.)

Names: Orr, Wendy, 1953-, author.
Title: Cuckoo's Flight / Wendy Orr.
Description: Toronto, Ontario Canada : Pajama Press, 2021. | Summary: "In Bronze-Age Crete, before horses were common on the island, potter's-daughter Clio continues to raise and train them even though an accident has left her unable to ride. After a series of difficult years in the community, the threat of raiders prompts the town's ruling Lady to demand the sacrifice of a maiden between ages twelve and fourteen, who will be selected at the spring equinox. Certain that she will be named the sacrifice, Clio struggles to go on with the ordinary activities of making pots and preparing the town's defenses. She finds refuge in her horses and a new friendship with younger girl Mika, who takes to riding as naturally as Clio did. Drawing on a spiritual connection with her grandmother Leira, Clio learns to believe that she has the power of choosing her path, and that she, Mika, and the horses may hold the key to saving the town without loss of life"— Provided by publisher.
Identifiers: ISBN 978-1-77278-190-8 (hardcover)
Subjects: LCSH: Bronze age -- Greece – Juvenile fiction. | Horsemanship -- Juvenile fiction. | Friendship – Juvenile fiction. | BISAC: JUVENILE FICTION / Historical / Prehistory. | JUVENILE FICTION / Animals / Horses. | JUVENILE FICTION / Disabilities & Special Needs.
Classification: LCC PZ7.O77Dr |DDC [F] – dc23

Cover and text: based on original design by Design by Committee
Cover and interior illustration: Josh Durham
Map illustration: Sarfaraaz Alladin, www.sarfaraaz.com

Manufactured by Friesens
Printed in Canada

Pajama Press Inc.
469 Richmond St. E, Toronto, ON M5A 1R1

Distributed in Canada by UTP Distribution
5201 Dufferin Street Toronto, Ontario Canada, M3H 5T8

Distributed in the U.S. by Ingram Publisher Services
1 Ingram Blvd. La Vergne, TN 37086, USA

To Olive and Claudia, Angus and Rose,
who will make their own history in a changing world.

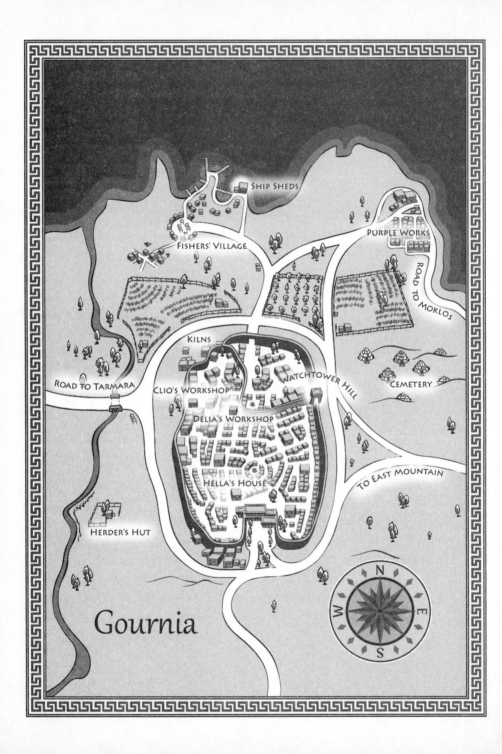

Gournia

If she had stayed to load the kiln as she should have, she'd never have seen the ship.

Mama said the ship would still have been there, so everything had to happen the way it did. But that's not true. Clio saw it, and the world changed.

CHAPTER 1
THE BLACK SHIP
IN WINTER

Selena's rules are strict: "Never, never, trust anyone else with our pots. We load them into the kiln ourselves and we take them out ourselves." And though Clio has to trust Head and Tail the carrier twins to take them from workshop to kiln, it's her job to follow the palanquin tray and check that nothing is damaged when it arrives.

The twins lower the poles to the ground. Smoothly as reflections in a mirror, they stoop again to lift the inner tray out onto a raised rock slab. Clio swings around it, keeping her crutch well out of the way. All the little figurines are upright and perfect.

"Goddess thank you," she says, hand on her heart. Tail passes her a soft clay tablet, and she stamps it with her grandmother's seal stone, hanging from a cord around her wrist.

But the kiln's lid is off and Delia is reaching in, just starting to take her own workshop's pots out.

"We can't wait for you to unload today," a twin says to Delia. It has to be Head because Tail never speaks. "We've got a load of spearheads for the palace from Igor the Bronze—we'll be back for your pots when we're done."

Delia and Clio try not to smile. They can fit more talk into firing a kiln than anyone would believe, but an excuse to take a little longer is a gift from the gods. Especially when Delia's bursting to finish the whispered story she started at the end of the dawn ceremony, about the priest girl who wants to marry a fisher boy—and how would the Lady ever let her do that?

"Though he's a pretty enough fisher to be descended from the sea god, and surely that's good enough even for priest-folk!"

Clio giggles. She wants to hear the story, and even more than that, she wants to simply be here with Delia, away from her family and the workshop. Sometimes it seems they understand each other as easily as the carrier twins.

But just as her friend is whispering about the fisher's secret visit to the palace, Clio feels a sudden tug at her heart, sharp as a jab of physical pain. The laughter dies in her throat.

Gray Girl! Her mare, dappled the color of the morning sea, is heavy with foal. "Any day now," Dada said yesterday, though it's earlier in the year than it should be, closer to winter than spring, and the rain is cold. Even if the grandmothers are right that winters aren't as cold or wet as they used to be, there's still enough ice in the air to chill a newborn foal. And her father will be busy all day in the shipsheds; he and Uncle Doulos want to finish repairing the hull and aren't even coming home for siesta. It'll be too late if Gray Girl is in trouble.

"You look like a mother with a sick babe!" says Delia. "Go—you won't be calm till you've seen her. I'll load your pots and start firing the kiln when I'm finished unpacking mine."

"We can't do that!"

It's true that for the last two years Delia has often helped her, because Clio needs to put her crutch down to lift the pots from the rock slab into the top of the kiln. She can balance on her stiff leg for a moment, though she's dropped more than one pot when she wobbles. What hurts more than the pain itself is needing the help. It's the one thing she can never tell Delia.

But helping is different from doing—and these are the goddess figurines, the specialty of her grandmother's workshop, not everyday cups or bowls. If Mama ever finds out...

"I'll be as careful as if they were my own," says her friend. "Selena will never know. I'll be waiting a while for the twins anyway."

"But..."

"You never know when I'll need a favor in return."

"A big one!" says Clio, wavering.

"A huge one," Delia agrees.

Clio is already swinging her way out to the river road, her crutch taking its giant strides and her stiff right leg lagging behind.

Gray Girl, misty as the morning sea,
   dappled like a pebbled beach,
   her heart beating with Clio's
   since they were raised, girl and foal,
   on the milk of the mare
   when Clio's mother had none.
Dada tells of lifting
   a babe too young to stand
   to the foal's back
   so they could learn each other's warmth
   and by the time they were two
   they moved as one.
Mama always afraid, saying that horses,
   wild as stags in the hills,
   had no place in their lives—
   but couldn't forbid
   because Dada's gods say
   they're the heart of his.
Clio wishes the goddess
   would say the same for her,
   but the Great Mother stays silent—
   except in the link she forged
   between horse and girl
   so that even that day,
   when a snake wriggled out from a rock
   through the mare's front legs
   so she shied and reared,
   throwing Clio hard to her knees—
   the left on the ground,
   the right onto the rock;

pain spearing into her hip
so fierce she thought she would die,
her mind closing in blackness—
Gray Girl wouldn't let her drown in that dark,
wouldn't leave her side,
standing guard on the path,
trumpeting a neigh of terror
till Petros the herder came,
and then Dada,
running all the way from town
and carrying Clio home
as if she were a babe.
She remembers Gray Girl's call
and seeing Dada's face drain
to the color of ash,
but nothing of the moon that followed
till she heard Mama weeping:
"Three daughters I've lost so far—
can the Great Mother not leave me one?"
And her grandmother's voice, calm and sure,
"The girl will live.
Her life will not be the one we planned
but when life changes
so must we—
and she is strong enough
to do that.'
Clio opened her eyes,
returned to life,
and her leg did its best to heal;
by winter she could stand

for a moment or two.
Hector carved a crutch—
now she can walk
nearly as fast as a run,
but the twisted leg
will not turn or grip the side of a horse—
she cannot ride.
Mama says that the snake,
the Great Mother's beast,
was clearly saying it was well past time
for Clio, an almost-woman,
to forget her horses
and turn her thoughts to her trade.
But Clio says her horse, born of the sea god,
showed respect for the Great Mother's snake
saved her life
and earned her gratitude.
They could argue about it all day
and sometimes do.
Dada never argues the ways of the goddess
but began to build
a chariot, like the ones from his home;
the harness first
so that long before the chariot was done
Gray Girl could begin to learn
the feel of this new skill.
Soft goat leather, stitched strong
over evenings into spring—
always out of Mama's sight—
for bridle, reins, chest band, and girth.

Returning from the sea in autumn
with fittings of bronze—
Mama so glad to see him safe and home
she couldn't complain;
shaped the poles,
built six-spoked wheels for strength—
like a war chariot, he said,
made to bounce over the roughest ground—
"Though I hope my child
will never need to go to war."
But the body has taken the longest of all
weaving basket after basket,
models for a doll—
a doll who cannot stand as a warrior does,
but must sit still
with her legs tucked safe.

The kilns are on the northwest corner of town, just outside the wall. In front of them the road to the sea winds between the barley field and the olive grove; on the left is the river road. Clio follows it to just before the washing rocks by the bridge, onto the smaller track to Gray Girl's valley.

Gray Girl's mother was a filly in her second summer when Hector arrived as a frightened fugitive on Uncle Doulos's ship. He saw wild horses as they came into the bay and knew that he could make a new life in this land; it was the first time he'd smiled since he punched a man for beating his horse, back home in Troy. He never tells the end of that story—all Clio knows for sure is that the young man who became her Dada fled to the sea and begged sanctuary from the captain of the first ship he saw. That captain was her mother's brother.

So, even before Selena married him, Clio's father had captured a filly, cared for her, and taught her to come to his whistle. He made a bridle of goat leather, and at the end of her third summer, when he came home from the trading season, trained her to carry him on her back.

After a while, when she tried to return to the wild herd she came from, the lead mare drove her away, though the stallion came down to visit her in the spring. She grew fat with a foal the second year, and the foal, when it was born, was fat and healthy too. But one morning, when Hector whistled for them, the mare came alone, ears laid back in fright, deep scratches on her legs and belly. He doesn't know what took the foal—wolves or wild dogs, or even shepherds jealous of the grass it ate—but he never saw a trace of it again. Most of the foals after that survived but found wild herds once they were grown—until three years ago, when Hector hired a family of goatherds to run the horses with their goats. The horses don't like the dogs, and if the horses go a different way than the flock the herders must choose their own goats, but they watch over them all as best they can.

The old mare died foaling last spring, so now there's just Gray Girl, her two-year-old filly Fleet

Foot, and the old mare's colt. He's coming in to his third spring, but he's still called Colti, because he's the last foal born.

Although Clio and her father say the horses are theirs, the truth is, even with Petros and his dogs guarding them, Gray Girl could lead her herd to freedom if she wanted. Clio sometimes thinks it's they who belong to the horses.

The giant vultures are wheeling high above now, scanning the ground for rotting flesh—and Clio's memory of the old mare's death turns into a vision of Gray Girl on the ground. Gray Girl lying alone, stranded and straining. The thought pulls her down the path faster than she's ever gone before, her crutch thumping through prickly bushes that scratch her leather apron and catch at her sheepskin cloak. She can't see any of the horses; or the goats or their herder.

At the top of the riverbank she stops long enough to catch her breath and whistle—a cuckoo's call: one long, one short. It's always brought Gray Girl from wherever she is. If she can walk.

The mare trots gently up the hill, her round belly swinging. The scent of trampled thyme reassures Clio before she sees her. Now soft lips are nuzzling the girl's face, whiskers tickling. Clio drops her crutch to stroke the mare's forehead, rub between her ears the way she loves, before running her hands over the round sides and belly. Everything feels normal.

"Thank you," she says, to the Great Mother and god of horses. Her right hand is on her heart in prayer, but she keeps her left on Gray Girl's face, to remind the gods who the thanks are for and from.

The colt and filly prance up but lose interest quickly when they see she hasn't picked anything for them. "Next time," she promises, though only Gray Girl's ears twitch as if she understands.

Clio buries her face against the warmth of the strong gray neck.

She knows she ought to hurry back to the kiln—*but I was so sure she needed me! What was that heart prickle if not Gray Girl's call?*

As if in answer, the mare nudges her shoulder. It's been two years now, but sometimes she forgets that her girl can't ride anymore.

"Even if I could," Clio tells her, "you're too near your time."

Gray Girl nudges again, and when Clio still refuses, starts up the hill.

Hector says that mares are often restless before they foal. *Is she searching for a safe place now?* Clio wonders. *Is that why I felt her calling?* She grabs her crutch again and follows.

The mare ambles up the hill to the ridge overlooking the river. The vultures have moved on, but eagles circle lazily in the winter sky; farther back toward town, Clio can see the goats grazing near the herders' hut. The tune of a flute wafts gently over the breeze. At the top of the ridge, Gray Girl stops and sniffs the wind.

On flat ground, the mare's shoulder is just above

the girl's chin. But here on the steep side of a hill, Gray Girl's back is level with her chest. It's almost overwhelmingly tempting to pull herself up, swing her left leg over and sit there, just for a moment, the way she used to…

She's tried often enough to know she can't. Even if her hip didn't scream with pain, the right leg doesn't turn to hug the mare's round barrel; it can't squeeze or grip. The only way she could stay on is to wrap her arms around the mare's neck—and that's not riding.

She wouldn't mind so much if she knew that her father's chariot idea would work. Maybe in his home in Troy, but what if there's a reason there's never been a horse-drawn chariot in this town?

"The reason is they're stuck in the past, thinking that only oxen can pull carts," Hector always says. "Once they understand how to make the new wheels, they'll see that horses can pull a light cart faster and farther than any ox."

"Is that true?" she asks the mare, resting her arms across the warm gray back and looking out over the blue waters of the bay. "Can we do it?"

That's when she sees it. A ship.

On this chill day of winter there shouldn't be a ship to see. There are more than two cycles of the moon before the sailing season begins; the little fishing boats go out in the bay, but the trading ships are safely in their sheds for the winter. Exactly as they should be.

But there, coming up to the east point of the bay, is a long black hull with a bright wicked eye at its bow and a bowsprit long and sharp as a swordfish's spike—and though there is breeze for a sail, the mast is down and the oars are flashing, stroke after even stroke.

The oars raise as if in salute, and when they lower again the ship disappears, going back the way it came from. It is the neatest turn she's ever seen.

Uncle Doulos would love to see that!

No, he wouldn't. No one wants to see that.

This isn't a trading ship from the next harbor. It's different from the island's ships: heavier, more rows of oars; the warlike eye instead of the gentle swallow of her uncle's ship or the octopus of his rival's. But the main difference is that they are out in the winter, rowing for no reason.

As if they're training. Training for the raiding season.

All this year, refugees have been coming in from villages farther up and down the coast. Warriors from the mainland started attacking when Clio's grandparents were young, in the dark days of fire and flood. The great sacrifice had given the goddess strength to hold them back for many years, but now they've started again. This time they don't seem satisfied with raiding, stealing, and slaving. Now they want the land too. The refugees tell of the villages they've invaded, the palaces and temples they've burned, and the farms they've taken. Say that some have beached their ships for winter in isolated coves and settled in as if they're going to stay forever.

But no one from the town has seen this proof till now. The raiders are closer than anyone's imagined, and they are readying themselves for war.

Gray Girl quivers beneath Clio's arms. *Is her time coming near? I need to get back to the kiln where I'm supposed to be—but I can't leave her if she's about to foal!*

The mare nuzzles the girl's face, asking her to blow into her nostrils in their private language, and Clio knows it's her own fear that Gray Girl is feeling, and that she's reassuring her as she would a foal. They share each other's breath for a long moment.

"Thank you," Clio whispers, and picks up her crutch.

The wind hits her as she moves away from the mare's bulk; she pins her cloak tighter around her shoulders but the shivering isn't just with cold. Stepping back down from this rock, she can't see the point at the end of the bay. If Gray Girl hadn't nudged her up to this particular slope of the hill, she wouldn't have seen the ship.

The thought hits hard as a stone to the belly. The ship didn't want to be seen.

And the other part of the thought: the goddess wanted her to see it.

I can't be the only one, she thinks desperately. *Goatherds will have seen it along the way.*

Maybe. But the lookout, up in the tower on the

eastern wall, won't have. If herders farther up the bay saw it, they'd think the town would see it too. By the time they tell someone, it might be too late.

Too late for what?

She doesn't want to think about that.

I'll tell the lookout, she decides, and then I won't have to tell Mama that I left the pots with Delia. Dada might understand, and even Grandmother Leira, but Mama is so worried about my future she's angry at everything I do that isn't exactly what she wants.

Deserting the kiln is a big one.

From the hill across the river
    Mika watches—
    the foal-bellied mare,
    the brown filly,
    and the prancing colt,
    taller and darker than the others—
    a wild beauty that makes her heart sing;
    watches the girl
    older than her by a year or three,
    lucky, well cared for and born to a craft—
    though Mika's visited town too rarely to guess
    more than she's neither priest-folk nor fisher;
    ponytail neat in a long dark plait,
    leather apron over her tunic
    and warm sheepskin as well.
But not so lucky in her legs
    for she drags the right
    and needs a crutch to stand.

She calls the horses with a cuckoo's song—
  they trot up like whistled dogs
  but the mare is the one she loves
  and the one that loves her—
  she strokes and leans on the round gray back
  as if she'll slide right on.
  "Do it!" wills Mika,
  longing to see the girl ride
  nearly as much as she yearns to do it—
  and when the horse girl stops,
  grabs her crutch and flees,
  Mika's bereft
  as if a warm meal
  has been snatched from her grasp.

CHAPTER 2
THE ORACLE

Delia is still at the kilns; she looks up from the fire, her face flushed and shocked to see her friend rush past without stopping.

"Back soon!" Clio calls.

She swings through the gate onto the cobbled street. This is the main craft quarter: small, two-storied whitewashed houses and workshops crowd on either side. It bustles with craft-folk, farmers, slaves, and priest-folk all going about their business; chatting, shouting orders, or singing as they work. Stone vase makers thump hammers; a dog barks frantically at a shepherd carrying a ram over his shoulders. The fresh salt scent of sea is overlaid by the stink of molten metal from the bronze workshop.

The carrier twins pass with a load of raw copper on their tray. "Igor said this was urgent," Head calls after her. "Your friend's pots are next."

Clio smiles back as if she hasn't been too worried to even wonder why they're just leaving now. At the corner, where Delia's mother's workshop is next to the weaver's, she turns and follows the narrow street up to Watchtower Hill.

The pacing lookout is tall and thin, a yellow shepherd's scarf wound around his dark hair. Petros. Clio flushes with warmth: she's guessed right. It was his sister fluting to the goats—her friend is on lookout duty.

"Clio! Are you lost? The kilns were down by the gate the last time I looked!"

He sees her face and the teasing stops.

"What's wrong?"

"I've seen a ship."

"How could you? I've been watching. I swear I didn't doze...maybe for a moment, no more. Don't tell anyone."

"I had a feeling Gray Girl was in trouble—I had to check. The ship was close in to shore and turned around at the point. You couldn't have seen it."

"I might have," he says. "And you might have been at the kilns, not out with the horses."

"But...oh! Thank you, Petros!"

As quickly as she can without knocking anyone over with her swinging crutch—dreading someone asking what she's doing at the lookout—Clio races back down the hill.

Delia is turning into her mother's workshop. She flashes a thumbs up and Clio thanks her with a hand-on-heart. No one else sees their quick signals.

She's still out of breath when she returns and tells Mama the figurines are firing now.

"You put them in facing east?"

Does Delia know that? Her family's workshop makes household dishes; Clio's is the only one that makes the house goddesses. But they've stacked the kilns together often enough.

Clio nods, trying to cool the red blush from her cheeks.

Mama pats her shoulder and pours her a cup of ale. "Rest; you're puffed out from stoking the fire."

Clio's blush blooms redder, from toes to scalp.

Matti, whose mother died giving birth to him four years ago, stops galloping his wooden goat around the floor and stares at his young aunt. "Why is Clio so red?" he demands.

Grandmother Leira, resting on her bed beside the shrine, watches Clio's face and says nothing.

"I'll check the mare with Clio before I go to the shipsheds," Hector says next morning.

"And me!" shrieks Matti, climbing his grandfather's leg as if it were a tree. "Take me too, Dada!" Hector and Selena are the only parents Matti's ever known— his father had died at sea soon after he was born. They think of him as their youngest child, Clio's little brother rather than her nephew.

"Not today," Hector says. "This is Clio's job. You help Mama with the clay."

Selena sighs. Her brother Doulos often complains

that Hector doesn't take the shipping seriously enough, and she can't see why it takes two people to check on one animal, especially when they pay a herder to do it…but there's no point in arguing with Hector or Clio when it comes to their horses.

Matti's wails fade as the Lady's call to the sun floats out from the palace courtyard. Clio and her father stop briefly to honor it, and turn onto the river road.

Petros is back with the flock today. "I haven't seen Gray Girl this morning," he says. "But Colti's restless, and I think he's guarding that hill."

The colt is near where Clio first saw the horses yesterday. He starts toward them before swerving up the ridge. Hector and Clio follow, hearts thumping anxiously till they hear a whickering and see the mare in a sheltered hollow near the bottom of the hill. She looks up at Clio's whistle and the shadow beside her becomes a perfect, healthy foal, paler than its mother, more the color of clay than her soft gray. Nuzzling into her side, the foal begins to nurse.

Gray Girl licks it protectively, still watching them.

"Thank you, Great Mother," Clio whispers.

Her father hugs her so hard she drops her crutch, and they both laugh. As they head back across the field, Clio sings and her father whistles.

Petros grins. "The foal is born?"

"Healthy mare and foal," Hector agrees. "Though they'll be wanting your protection in these next days."

Petros nods. "We'll keep the goats in this field till at least the next turning of the moon. The only problem would be if she gets through the barrier at the shallow ford. It's stood all winter, but not if she's determined to get through."

"She loves to wade there, even when it's cold," says Clio. "And if she wants to keep her foal away from the goats…"

"We'll repair it now," says Hector.

"I'll take them down to water with the goats every night, and the foal will get used to the flock from the start," says Petros.

The gully at the river's bend
   carved from the steep bank
   washes silt to the water
   trapping pebbles from the creek above—
   gravel and silt forming a ledge
   across the river, nearly to the other shore.
But that far bank
   is steep with rocks,
   not easy even for goats—
   and unwary beasts
   wading on that peaceful ledge
   can be swept away when they step
   into the river's depth.
Now the goats follow Petros
   like children in a game,
   a favorite bumping at his heels
   while others wander—
   searching always for something better—
   but all watching

where their herder goes,
especially when he starts to cut
thorny branches that they might eat.
Hector chops with Petros
while Clio, sheepskin pinned tight at the throat
snaps off two long thorns
to pin the cloak at each wrist,
shielding her arms with tough hide sleeves —
and weaves new fence into the old.
It's not a task anyone could love —
face-slapping branches escape their weave,
thorns tear fingers, stab through capes
and seek bare legs, keen as hunters —
but between yowls and sucking bloodied fingers,
Clio sings the joy of her heart,
of working in the fresh cold air
with her father and friend
rather than home on the workshop floor,
where time moves slowly —
clay slipping, oozing through her fingers,
refusing to be shaped —
even these sharp thorn branches
love her more than the clay.
The fence can be crooked
but as long as it works
she has not failed.

Building the barrier will keep the foal safe, but a few
days later, when Clio opens the cooled kiln, it seems
the goddess herself has blessed the birth.

Every little figurine—a head and torso with raised arms on a skirt like an upturned cup—is perfect, and facing east.

Clio can't apologize to Delia for that niggling doubt, but wishes she could leave the carrier twins, busy loading their palanquin tray to return the figurines to the workshop, to thank her friend again.

"As soon as they're all safely stored," she promises herself.

But there's much more to talk about by then.

Everyone, from the lowest slave to the Lady and the goddess herself, knows about the ship Clio saw three days ago. Now it's leaked out that it wasn't Petros who saw it from the watchtower but Clio from the ridge with her horses.

I should have just told Mama the truth then!

Her mother's scolding is soon the least of her worries. At the next morning's dawn ceremony, the Lady announced that she would consult the oracle. Now it is noon and the townfolk have returned to hear what the goddess demands to save them from this new danger.

From the palace balcony
    the Lady appears,
    gold at her throat and wrists,
    tall coned hat,
    tight-laced blouse,
    and a flounced skirt bright
    with the gods' own purple.

Face-paint death white,
   lips red as blood
   and huge eyes glazed
   from communing with gods,
   reading the patterns on a grain-dusted floor
   where the Great Mother's snake
   chases fleeing mice.
Swaying, gazing
   over the silent crowd;
   her goddess voice
   is hoarse and deep.
"The oracle says the need is great:
   these warriors, men of bronze
   on black ships bright with shields and spears,
   threaten not only homes and lives
   but the goddess herself, mother of all,
   casting her out where she lives
   in statues of clay or wood,
   for their jealous gods of sky and sea,
   thunder and war,
   and the bull who shakes the earth.
"The wounded goddess calls for the blood
   of the great sacrifice, last given long ago—
   a promise there will always be
   women to serve her
   so she can care for
   her people on earth.
"The day of the spring festival
   when the moon rises full
   after the heavens balance light and dark

so night lasts just as long as day—
we will offer a ram,
a she-goat, and a yearling calf—
then a sacrifice for no one's feasting—
pure gift to the goddess.
A maiden—
a girl, an almost-woman—
to go down to the dark earth
of the Great Mother's body
and live with the goddess there."
Clio hears her father gasp,
sees Delia pale,
feels her mother shudder
and her own heart race.
All through Clio's life she's heard
of the sister her mother never met
Grandmother Leira's first-born daughter,
chosen in dark days of drought and hunger
to live with the gods.
She's heard of the honor,
of how the townfolk opened their hearts,
brought gifts of food and household help,
an apprentice to work the clay
in the departed girl's place,
and most of all, praise
for the work that continued
in her life underground
as the relenting gods
brought rain and harvest again to the land.
She's heard the story from her mother,

from neighbors and grannies around the town;
only her own grandmother—
and grandfather Andras when he was alive—
never speak of it
or shed a tear at the sound of the name.
Sometimes,
on days when her hip jabs sharp,
Clio envies this unknown aunt,
forever a girl in her life underground
free from pain and daily cares,
a priestess in the gods' dark home,
her grave honored at every feast.
But now it seems
this girl's work is done
and the goddess needs another.
Day turns to night:
the sun disappears;
silence whispers over town,
shock heavy as mud.
And Clio wishes she'd never
seen that ship.

For days no one can talk of anything else. The Lady's words swirl endlessly in Clio's mind; being with the horses is the only way she can stop them. Even then she has to avoid Petros, in case he wants to talk about it.

Will she see people she's known in the peaceful world of the afterlife? She'd be glad to tell her sister that the son she died birthing is a beautiful boy, clever and kind, and how he loves the clay. And she'll be glad not to limp, because she'll be free of pain in the home of the gods.

Or will she be forever at the shrine, doing whatever a priestess would do? Collecting the blood of sacrifices offered from the earth above, to offer the goddess in a golden cup? Singing her praises—or dancing her praises, since she won't need a crutch anymore? Apart from that, Clio simply can't imagine.

Which doesn't stop her picking at the thought like an itching scab.

"Will you help Mama train a new apprentice?" she asks Delia. "Matti is too small to be much use yet."

"You don't know it's going to be you!" Delia snaps. "The Lady said the girl would be chosen by lot and there are fourteen of us the right age—it could be anyone."

"I know," Clio mutters, "I was just asking in case!" She hurries home before her hurt and anger spill out into friendship-smashing words.

But how can Delia not understand? It's Clio's family's story; her aunt who has to be replaced. The fact that she's the one who saw the ship simply seals their fate.

Grandmother Leira wakes next morning,
    sits up in her bed shouting, "No!"
    in a voice to make them run,
    fear in their hearts—
    but Leira's eyes are shining bright
    and her voice is strong.
"I have a plan," she says, holding Clio close,

"You are the gift of a gift—
for your mother bore you
later than she thought she could,
as I did with her—
so it's no surprise
the goddess has destined you for honor.
And it's not for us mortals to complain:
but not this way, Great Mother, not this way."
An oracle's message
has more than one reading, she says—
and though Leira is not a priestess,
the secret everyone knows
is that she was priest-folk
long ago in her land that died.
And perhaps being the mother
of the last girl to serve
gives her words more weight.
So when she goes to the palace,
her stick tap-tapping on the stones
a slower rhythm than Clio's following crutch—
Clio and Selena afraid to speak—
the Lady comes out to the courtyard
and listens.
The oracle could also mean,
says Grandmother Leira,
looking straight into the Lady's eyes,
that the goddess needs
a priestess who can never die
but will always serve.
"This is what I'll create,"

she says,
"and if the goddess lets me live that long
we can know she approves."
The Lady cannot say no
but doesn't say yes.
"Make your statue and guard it
with the vigil of a newborn babe.
The oracle will decide
when the full moon rises
on the eve of the rites of spring—
you will bring it to me then
but not before."
So Grandmother Leira,
so old and frail
the breath rattles in her chest,
returns to the clay
and the wheel she'd left for her daughter
and Clio.
Working from sunrise till eve,
this day and the next
and another three;
she creates a statue,
a woman no taller
than Clio's elbow to wrist,
with the skirts and apron of priesthood,
a goddess snake clasped in each hand,
and a face so clear and lifelike
it could almost breathe.
She sets it aside to dry
and makes another

until there are four in a row;
pounds quartz
into the finest powder;
mixes color in different hues,
not satisfied until the day
the first statue is dry as a bone
and ready to glaze.
Refusing help even from Mama
she carries them to the kiln herself
sets the fire
and stokes it all night,
sleepless by its side,
not returning to her bed
till the fire is done—
barely breathing
through the days of cooling,
until she pulls open the heavy lid
to lift the statues from the kiln.
Brilliant in turquoise and green,
they are perfect and whole,
though only the first-made shines with life.
Leira places it on the home shrine
beside the house goddess
and smashes the others
as offering to it.
But it seems her own breath
was mixed into the glaze,
absorbed in the firing,
for that very night
Leira dies.

CHAPTER 3
LEIRA'S FAREWELL

Clio can't imagine life without her grandmother. She knows that only the gods live forever and that all other living creatures—birds, beasts and people, dragonflies and dolphins—will return to the Great Mother one day. She knows she's lucky to have had a grandmother till she was nearly grown, especially being the youngest-by-far of her youngest-by-far daughter.

Nothing makes it any easier.

Not my grandmother! Clio wants to say. *She's survived so much in her life, why couldn't she defeat death too?*

Because Grandmother Leira was a slave before she made pots, but before she was a slave she was a priestess girl, rich with gold and slaves of her own—till the gods destroyed her land. Her sea captain father brought her and her injured mother to this Great Island, to their kin at the palace of Tarmara—but a great wave destroyed that town too, and she fled here. She endured enough for a hundred lifetimes.

The whole town mourns. People who Clio barely knows, who she's never seen visit her grandmother, come to the house to farewell her. It seems that Leira, who came to this town as an unwanted refugee with only her grandmother and injured mother, has touched more lives than anyone could imagine. Some people say she's the reason that, after the great sacrifice, the oracle proclaimed that from now on the town would always welcome fleeing strangers.

Delia cries with Clio and their mothers hug as tightly as the girls. Delia's great-grandmother Teesha was an apprentice with Leira, and her first friend—apart from Andras, who became Clio's grandfather. The families have been interwoven ever since. Old Granny Pouli, the winemaker across the road who has argued with Leira about anything and nothing since before anyone else can remember, is weeping so hard she needs two grandsons to keep her upright for the few steps between their houses.

Even the Lady, still unable to admit that Leira had once been priest-folk, sends a messenger with a jug of wine to honor the woman who'd given her daughter to save the town.

The gods give them a mild and sunny winter's morning for the funeral. The cemetery is at the bottom of the mountain, just outside the eastern wall—Clio thinks that when they greet the sun each morning, they'll be greeting her grandmother too. Better to think of sunrise than the frail body tucked into the painted clay chest Hector, Uncle Doulos, and two of Clio's male cousins are carrying.

Selena and Clio follow, wailing the high lu-lu-lu of mourning; little Matti is crying too hard to walk and Selena carries him, though tears stream down her face too. The mountain rises steep and green, the bay sparkles blue, and the line of chanting, keening people behind the family stretches from the grave to the town wall.

Farewell to life,
the sun and sky,
Farewell to toil,
to sea and soil.
Your days are done
your life here gone;
for now you rest
in our mother's breast.
Live with her there
and leave us here.

On the hill to the north, behind the purple works, a small group of people dressed only in loincloths stand watching—slaves risking a beating to farewell the woman who has become a legend to them. Although generations of slaves have lived and died since Leira escaped that terror, she is remembered still because of those she's helped throughout the years. When times were good with the pots and the gold flowed in, she would trade for a slave from the purple works. They'd work in the pottery workshop long enough to grow strong in their bodies and fierce in their hearts, learning that they were human and not beasts. Some became apprentices; some sailors, and others moved on to different crafts or far-off towns.

Every once in a while, a traveling merchant or peddler will come to the door with a gift to thank Leira for the life returned, whether to them or the far-away worker who'd once been a slave.

And always, when a slave came with a sledge full of dried shells to be baked and crushed and mixed into the clay, Leira would honor them as if they were any other human. Clio had learned early that she mustn't gag at that nauseating stench, and instead must offer ale to drink, and a barley cake or dried figs to eat.

"Do you think they like it?" Her grandmother had demanded, her voice strident with passion. "Do you think it's their choice to live as worse than dogs? We can't free them all, but while they are in our workshop, they will have a few moments of being treated as if they were free." And she'd repeat the irony that the prized purple dye of the priest-folk, in their town and all around the world, was created by such putrid shellfish that the slaves who worked there were outcasts because of the smell that became part of them. The only time they were allowed through the town gates was to haul the sledges of empty shells— which is how Leira herself had found her way into the pottery studio.

They bury the chest at the edge of a rock shelter, where Leira's parents, grandmother, and husband Andras lie buried, as well as Clio's older sisters—Matti's mother and two who died as babies—and aunts, uncles, and cousins she never knew or can hardly remember.

Faces smeared with the ashes and tears of mourning, the townfolk cry for Leira but sing for them all. They sing the story of Leira's life and death. Seagulls join in with plaintive cries while higher up, eagles circle and watch in silence. Clio wishes for the swallows that her grandmother loved, but it'll be another two cycles of the moon before they return for spring.

I'll tell her when they do, she thinks. *If I'm still above the ground.*

Uncle Doulos lays a bleating lamb on the altar stone. Aunt Fotia, Grandmother Leira's oldest living daughter, slices its throat and Selena catches the blood in a painted chalice, pouring it onto the grave to feed her mother in the afterlife.

Through the trance of grief, Clio feels herself lifted out of her body; she becomes one with the lamb and feels the cold blade on her throat. *No, no, no!* her mind shrieks, so loudly she's surprised no one else hears.

Clio has seen sacrifices all her life—but this is the first one since the oracle. The first time she's thought about the creature giving its life to honor the gods and feed the family. The first time she's thought about how the chosen maiden would pass from this world to the next. She doesn't want to be that lamb; doesn't want to lie on a cold altar stone or to have her blood trickle anywhere, even into the goddess' shrine.

She doesn't even care about being free of pain and her crutch; she doesn't care about the honor of serving the Great Mother. She wants the earth and sky; she wants to laugh with Delia and Petros and all their friends; to see little Matti grow; to be with her horses and learn to drive the chariot her father is so painstakingly building. She even wants to work in the studio with her mother—because who else can do it and what will happen to the work of her grandmother and mother's lives if she isn't there to carry it on?

Her only hope now is to keep the priestess statue safe, and pray that her grandmother can petition the goddess to accept it.

With a small sharp rock, she slashes her arm and lets the blood drip onto the grave. "You gave your last breath to keep me from being the sacrifice. I vow that I will do all I can to honor your wish; to tell you of all that happens; and to listen for your guidance."

As if the gods have planned Leira's death for maximum honor, the feast of the household goddesses is the next day. From palace to smallest cottage, images of clay, wood, or stone come out to be paraded around the town and fields, calling the earth to begin to awaken for spring.

"I'll take the goddess," says Clio's mother, "but you will carry the priestess statue."

Clio's blood chills with fear. "I can't! What if I drop it?"

"You won't," Selena says firmly. "You can't, and you won't. We need to show the statue the town she'll protect—and it needs to be you who takes her."

Because it's you whose place she'll take. Selena doesn't say that, but Clio hears it just as clearly.

She has never hated her crutch more. She's never feared tripping more—it's terrifyingly easy to trip with a crutch, for the tip of the stick to catch between uneven cobblestones, to bump it against a wall and lose balance. *Drop the crutch if you start to fall!* she orders herself. *Fall on your back and keep the statue safe!*

She doesn't fall. She doesn't even stumble. They join the parade in front of the great white walls of the palace courtyard, follow the street looping below the wall and out the gate, around the barley field on the left; the olives on the right and the field of peas and lentils beyond. Clio's voice is still hoarse from weeping and her chest tight with tension, but she rasps out the song of awakening and tells the statue of all they're passing, even the rock shelter in the cemetery where the statue's creator lies.

The day is cool, drizzling the good omen of a light rain as they reach the barley fields. Only Clio's tunic is stained with sweat. *If I drop the priestess, Grandmother Leira will have died for nothing.*

They haven't eaten since last night. After the sun sets there'll be barley cakes and a dish of peas and lentils, washed down with ale—a reminder to the goddess of all that needs to be awakened in the dark earth of her body. But if the Great Mother herself had offered Clio the sweetest sip of honey mead, her throat would have closed against it till the statue was safely home.

Then, into this day of holiness comes an octopus hunter. He's not one of the town's own fishers, but is following the procession trying to peddle a pole-full of dangling octopus. Clio is too intent on carrying her statue to notice him, but the other townfolk are not so blind.

"Barbarian!" they hiss. "Bringing fish to this fast day! Get out before you offend the goddess and curse our crops!"

The man is small and wiry with ink-stained hands. A flung stone hits his shoulder, and he whirls around, his face livid with humiliation and rage.

"It's not stones you need to worry about!" shrieks the oldest woman he's ever seen, sitting outside a wine-maker's house. "Your blasphemy has cursed our crops and now I curse you!

> *"First your eyes and then your teeth*
> *one by one your limbs grow weak.*
> *To atone the ill luck made*
> *Gods demand a high price paid:*
> *Fear will spread its deathly pall*
> *and into slavery you will fall."*

The fisher spits. If he were braver he'd spit in the old woman's face—but he isn't. His gob of phlegm lands harmlessly behind a girl carrying a statue that is different from all the other goddesses: ornate, lifelike, and obviously precious. It doesn't look as if it should belong to the workshop the girl turns into, across the street from the old cursing woman.

Vowing vengeance, the octopus fisher strides back down the river road.

Mika waits under a tree on the other side of the bridge. She trembles as she watches her brother returning; she can see his anger long before his face is clear. When she realizes that he's still carrying all the octopus, her stomach clenches till she nearly vomits.

He'd wanted her to go into the town with him—sometimes people will buy better from a child than a man—but Mika hasn't been to town since their mother died four years ago. Her fear irritates him, and when Dymos is irritated, it quickly turns to rage.

"Just stay here and hide if you're so scared! No one's going to buy from that sniveling face!"

So she'd stayed under the tree, and she didn't have to hide, because there's no one washing clothes at the gravelly place beside the bridge and no one else has gone past. It was the best morning's fishing he'd had for longer than she can remember; he'd even sung with her on the way over instead of shouting at her to stop hurting his ears. She wondered what he'd trade for and hoped it was dried barley or something they could cook. The first time he'd sold the catch himself after their father died, he'd traded it for wine. He'd drunk it all that night, without adding any water, and was so sick that she thought he was going to die too. Her brother is all the family she has left and the only thing she's more afraid of than Dymos himself is the thought of him dying. Their aunt had died a moon before their father in the sickness last winter, along with six other people in their little settlement. Mika's friend, the only other girl her age, survived but her mother has taken her farther west to Tarmara in hopes of finding work and a better life. Now there are only four families left, and Mika knows that without her brother, she'd be no better than a slave to whichever family took her in.

She stands, rocking from one foot to the other—she wants to run home ahead of him but it might make him even angrier. He strides past without slowing, jerking his head at her to follow.

"It's some sort of holy day," he hisses. "They'll eat tonight but they won't touch any meat or fish till after sunrise tomorrow. Idiots!"

"I can dry them when we get back," Mika offers, and immediately wishes she could swallow the words. Octopus dry quickly on a line in the summer, but not when it's cold and drizzling like it is right now.

"Do you not have the brains of a dead jellyfish?" he spits. "Do you think we can sell them when they're rotten and stinking?"

Mika doesn't suggest that they could cook and eat them, share them with the settlement, and hope to trade the rest tomorrow already roasted, though she hopes that's what they'll do.

He turns on her as if she's said it anyway. "We're never trading here again! I'd rather trade with the real barbarians than give this town another fish!"

In this time of grieving
    it seems Grandmother Leira
    lives in the statue she created:
    this bright-robed priestess,
    her face like a younger Selena—
    or an older Clio.
Sometimes
    keeping vigil alone, eyes tear-wet,
    Clio wonders if she's praying
    to her grandmother
    or the goddess.
    Her head whirls with sadness—
    Grandmother Leira knew her
    as no one else does
    for though she had many grandchildren
    Clio's always been sure
    that secretly
    her grandmother loved her best.
So she grieves
    with the wail of mourning,
    ash on her face,
    blood on her arm,
    but most of all
    in her heart.

And even as she sings praise
    dark guilt floods her soul,
    wondering if her grandmother gave
    her own life for hers.
Selena, voice raspy with keening,
    says that Leira lived a long full life
    and deserves to rest
    in the afterlife now—
    but Clio would rather have her here.
She remembers Leira's stories—
    how excited she was to make the feast cups,
    the first things she'd made after being a slave
    and always after, every time she made them,
    four times a year all the years since then,
    she was still flooded with that hope and joy:
    "A simple cup but a sacred task," she'd say.
In reward she was sent a vision—
    a goddess statue, simple and quick
    cheap enough for every family to own
    and easy to teach her daughters:
    the upturned cup the bell of a skirt,
    adding a simple torso and head,
    worshipping arms outstretched.
Clio tries
    to honor her grandmother in the work of the clay,
    making cup after simple cup
    to be used and smashed
    in the great rites to come,
    though all she wants is to flee
    and if she could ride

she'd go far into the hills,
wild and alone.
Her mother slides clay through her hands
singing mud into beauty,
but Clio's slip and slide on the wheel
possessed by demons
and her mother cries in wonder
that she could have a daughter
so unfriendly to clay.
Though Grandmother Leira used to say,
"The gods don't always decree
a daughter will follow her mother's steps,"
even though she knew—
better than anyone—
their family wouldn't exist
without the pots.
Because when her sea captain father
returned to Tarmara after the flood,
no one knew where Leira had gone
or if she was alive.
He searched each season
for his lost wife and daughter
but did not find them till
she became mistress of her craft,
earning the right to stamp her pots
with the seal Grandpa Andras made—
a swallow flying over a crocus—
sending them out to the world to trade,
where they found her father
and he found his family.

During the winter, Hector works with Uncle Doulos most mornings to get the ship ready for the spring sailing. After siesta he helps to haul clay or pack finished pots; sometimes he hunts and brings home a hare, an agouti goat, or even a stag for dinner—those days he's the hero of the family instead of Selena's slightly strange husband—because in his homeland all the horsemen hunted.

But with his old mare dead, Hector hunts on foot this year. He's slid onto Colti's back to let him feel the weight and has trained him to wear the bridle, but it will be another year or more before the horse can gallop through brush with his rider shooting arrows from a bow.

"He's ready to be ridden, but it'll be harder to work through any bad habits if I start now and don't ride again till I get home. The same with Gray Girl—we'll go slowly as she learns that you can control her from the chariot just as you did when you rode."

But the chariot isn't finished yet, so on rainy afternoons and sometimes sunny ones, Hector works on it. He wants to finish it as soon as he can so that he can train Gray Girl to pull it and Clio to drive before he leaves for the sailing season. The mare was surprised the first time Clio bridled her and didn't get on her back, but she is now used to the man and girl walking behind her, Clio guiding with her voice while her father uses the long reins. Gray Girl's ears twitch as she walks; she's an intelligent horse and Clio is sure she's wondering why she doesn't just get on and ride.

How I'd love to! thinks Clio. Yet despite that ache of longing, there's something soothing in watching the movement of the horse in front of her, from that round gray rump and swishing tail to the perked, sensitive ears. Her heart is lighter and the clay flows smoother when she returns to the workshop.

It flows best of all when her father is with them, working on the chariot. He sings sagas of the horsemen of his land: stories of courage in war or the thrill of a race, horses and chariots lined up to fly at the starter's shout. He tells of the bonds between horses and their riders or charioteers—and Clio knows he's trying to convince her that a driver can feel the same freedom, the same power and thrill as a rider. She doesn't believe him.

But she does believe the stories about the place of horses in their clans. "Folk with horses are powerful," he says, "and not just because of war and races. We'll always need oxen for heavy loads, but a horse can be ridden or driven, or take a light load faster and farther. One day this land will believe it."

Flashes of joy through dreams
   feeling the thunder of hooves,
   wind in her face,
   and the rocking rhythm
   of the horse she rides
   till mare and girl are one.
Breathing in warm horse-sweat smell,
   feeling the tickle

of warm gray barrel
beneath her legs.
So real the grief of waking
is quickly gone
and the feeling comforts her
through the day.

Mika dreams the same, even though she's never experienced it and the horsehair that she pictures is so dark it's almost black.

The other difference is that she wakes with a tingle of excitement instead of grief, though her brother's seething anger quickly changes it to fear. He's still raging with resentment about his humiliation in the town.

Mika stays out of the way of his words and fists as much as she can, wading into the shallows with her net for small fish in the first light of the sun, levering sea urchins and limpets off rocks with her small stone knife, before heading to the hills for early spring greens. She never tells Dymos that the search takes her across the river from where the three horses run with a herd of goats. She doesn't tell of how she watches from her hiding place, studying the way the man slides onto the brown horse's back or of how she practices the girl's cuckoo whistle to call the horses.

CHAPTER 4
THE SPYING GIRL

Ever since the oracle,
    Clio feels her mama watching—
    watching as if she thinks
    her daughter will disappear
    and only the rope of her careful eyes
    will keep Clio from flying
    away into nothingness—
    as if she doesn't trust Leira's statue
    to serve the goddess
    instead of a sacrificed girl.
Tonight, returning from the privy,
    Clio hears her parents from the door,
    Hector saying, "She could come with me—
    stay safe at sea
    until this cursed season is past."
Selena laughs, hard and bitter,
    "You've never before said 'safe at sea',

my man who hates the waves.
The god of the sea is wild and fierce,
that's what you've said.
The ship is small and the waves are tall,
that's what you've said,
with slave-seeking pirates on every shore."
But most dangerous of all,
says Clio's mother,
would be to cheat the goddess
or thwart her will.
Better to appease her
as Leira planned and the Lady agreed—
to show our trust
in the clay priestess that took my mother's
breath,
than risk the anger
that knows no bounds."
Clio wishing she hadn't heard,
not wanting to know their fears
choosing to wonder instead—
who would watch over the horses
if she were off with her Dada?
And though her blood thrills
to think of freedom
from clay and chores
her bones know
she belongs to this land.

While the families of twelve- to fourteen-year-old girls
worry about the coming sacrifice, the palace and guards

are more concerned with the raiders. In fact, everyone is worrying about a raid. Fear hangs over the town like a storm cloud over the sea, pressure building as if the thunder god is waiting to tantrum. The only things flying faster than the chief's orders are the rumors—and the only thing the rumors have in common is that each of them adds to the terror.

The west wall needs rebuilding, the chief announces.

"They've just noticed?" Hector mutters, and Petros says the same: "Any goat could have told you that."

But they say it quietly. This is not the time to anger the palace.

The other walls are also being strengthened, and that means work parties from every quarter. As well as their days on lookout duty, all healthy men and boys—and all women who aren't pregnant or feeding babies—will leave their own work one day in four to collect rocks for the stonemasons to build with.

The exceptions are the bronze workers, who will be busy forging and sharpening spearheads and daggers; the stone workers, who are to switch from creating vases to axes—and the pottery workshops. The latter becomes less surprising after next morning's dawn ceremony, when the sun has risen above the east mountain and the Lady's last song has died away.

"The Lady has consulted the oracle," the chief booms, before everyone starts chattering and thinking about breakfast.

Silence falls like a cloak over the crowd. The Lady leaves her wooden stage in the courtyard and reappears on the palace balcony, where they all have to gaze up at her.

"Without trade, our town will die. Our land is not rich in metals; we must sail over the seas to exchange our goods for the copper and tin we need to create our bronze. The ships will sail for the trade route before the spring festival—earlier than usual, to secure the best goods in exchange and bring wealth to our town. But our good bronze weapons are not for trading, or our strong stone axes. The ships will be loaded with our fine purple fabrics, the luxuries of jewellery, stone vases and figurines, and most of all, with our pottery, which is equaled by none in the world and trades well in all places."

There isn't much time. To create, dry, and fire takes half a turning of the moon, and the spring festival is less than two moons away now. The goddess hasn't yet determined the exact date of sailing, the Lady continues—Clio sees her father share a wry look with Uncle Doulos: *You don't need an oracle to read the wind and weather*, she's often heard him say. *Pay attention to the sea and it will tell you what you need to know.*

For the first time, Clio realizes that although Hector hadn't willingly chosen the sea, he's been a sailor for five-and-twenty years, and it's part of him. If Uncle Doulos didn't have sons he might have become a captain. *Maybe he'd like it even more then,* she thinks.

But this year everyone is thinking the same thing: *so*

many men to leave our town at a time of danger! What if the raiders come?

"The Great Mother bids us," the Lady concludes, "to prepare for both peace and war. We plan for the offerings created from our wealth but will also be ready to repel any threat to our town."

Her voice grows stern, losing its mystical tone. "She bids you all follow the orders of the chief and the guards. You will work as they demand; you will give as they demand—and this is how you will please the goddess."

The crowd is silent as it troops out of the courtyard.

Selena is home with the statue this morning. Clio, Matti and Hector have gone to the ceremony together, but now Hector is walking with Doulos, heads close, and Clio and Matti are with Delia and her mother.

"We're lucky," Delia whispers. "At least we can go on with our work instead of digging out rocks."

"And it makes it easier to for someone to always be with the statue," Clio adds. "But I wish…"

I wish the Lady had taken it to the shrine when it was finished. I wish the oracle could have decided then. The weight of looking after it is crushing us.

She doesn't say it. Best not to criticize the goddess, or the oracle, or the Lady who is their mouthpiece. Bad enough even to have the thought.

Besides, she loves the statue. It's not just beautiful—it's a part of her grandmother, still there with them. She will miss it when it moves to the shrine.

And if doesn't move to the shrine, then I will. Or will we both go? I hope so. I would want it there with me.

"We'll have to work out timings for the kilns," says Delia's mother, turning down Clio's street with her.

Selena is waiting anxiously. She'd heard the long pause between the dawn songs finishing and the rumble of feet leaving the palace courtyard. She knew that something important was being said.

Delia's mother fills her in quickly. "The ships are to leave early."

"Dada is with Uncle Doulos now," Clio adds.

Her mother's eyes fill with sudden, unexpected tears. She brushes them away impatiently with the back of her hand. "I'd hoped that perhaps—with the fear of raiders—the palace would want them to stay; to have the men here to fight."

"The oracle said that without trade our town dies. And we know that's true."

"Without our men to fight, it may be us that die," Selena mutters. She looks at her friend's shocked face and is instantly contrite. It's less than a year since Delia's father died; there'll be no man in their home, no matter what the ships do. The two women hug each other tight for a moment.

"What are they crying about?" Matti asks Clio.

"Dada will be going on his ship soon."

"Can I go too?"

"No. He'll be gone a long time."

"I don't want him to go a long time!" Matti bellows.

"I don't want him to go with Grandmother Leira! I want him here!"

"He's not going underground—he'll come back," Selena reassures him.

"And the guards will protect us," Delia's mother reassures her.

Selena nods, and they begin to work out a schedule for the kilns and how to repair the old one that hasn't been used for years. They'll need all the kilns firing to have everything done early.

Time rushes,
    the moon spinning fast
    and the racing sun eager
    to get to his bed each night.
The townfolk race with him
    in their craft or on the wall,
    so the streets hum louder
    with the thumping of rocks,
    hammers banging on stone
    clanging on metal,
    and the hiss of hot bronze
    as it hits cold water.
    There are shouts and cries, bellows and shrieks
    but not so much singing.
Hector and Doulos have studied their goods
    the chief himself checking
    that no weapons will leave
    and which goods will be best
    for the sake of the town.

And at last Clio learns
  to shape the statues for small home shrines
  because the Lady believes
  they will show the world this town is sacred
  and not to be plundered.
"Aren't you proud?" Delia asks.
  "I knew you were skilled—
  now your mama sees it too."
But Clio wonders if Mama
  would have believed in her skill
  without the Lady's demands,
  and though she tries
  to think of her grandmother
  each time she throws clay on her wheel
  and to ask the Great Mother's blessing
  for the small sacred figures
  at the end of the day it sometimes feels
  no more than making feast cups
  to be used and smashed.
She wouldn't mind if only
  there was more time for the horses—
  to see Fouli growing from day to day,
  groom Fleet Foot to keep her tame,
  watch Dada ride Colti
  and most of all
  to learn with Gray Girl
  how to drive the chariot
  before Hector leaves.
But it must wait
  for the ships to be ready

and even when they are done
Hector takes his turn
digging rocks for the wall,
and one day rides Gray Girl
to distant farms
calling boys to adventures at sea.
"Could we not use
men from the purple?"
he and Doulos ask the chief.
But the chief says no
because what will happen
when they face pirates or thieves—
sailors must be armed
but how can a slave be trusted
with a knife or spear?
The purple works can send
slaves to dig rocks for the wall
at siesta time, when the sun is hot
and free folk must rest.
But sailors, to be loyal and brave,
will be chosen from folk of town and field.

Five days after the oracle, the Lady decrees that the ships will sail next morning. Any goods that aren't ready—pots that aren't fired, bronzes not polished—can wait. The ships' holds are filled, she says, and the trading season has begun.

It's never been so early. When Clio's grandparents were young, it didn't start till the spring festival, after the equinox. This year, it's still twenty-one days till that night of balance, and another twenty-one till the full moon after. *Forty-two days*, thinks Clio. *Is that how long I have to live?*

Matti howls again when he hears. Clio hugs and comforts him; inside she wants to howl too.

Hector's attached the poles to the finished chariot. It's standing on end on the outdoor workshop floor, and it is beautiful. The wickerwork basket is open in front, with a floor of tightly woven strips of leather. But instead of standing like a war charioteer, Clio will sit, with her legs resting on a frame in front. The whole thing is so light she can drag it with one arm.

"I'll be your horse," says her father, standing between the poles. "Get in!"

"Me too!" calls Matti, but Hector and Clio say no in one voice. "I'll take you when I know how to drive," Clio adds.

"After I come back on the ship," says Dada.

Matti's bottom lip quivers. Hector can never bear to see the little boy cry. He lifts him onto his shoulders and gallops out through the workshop to the street, snorting and neighing.

Matti laughs so hard he's nearly as out of breath as Hector by the time they stop.

"Are you the child or the grandfather?" Selena demands, but she is smiling as she lifts Matti down.

"It's a lucky child who grows to be a grandparent, but every grandparent was once a child," Hector answers—a not-answer to a not-question, that sounds like something the oracle might pronounce.

"Now it's Clio's turn," he says.

"She can't go on your shoulders!" Matti shrieks.

"Clio," says Hector, "is going in the chariot."

Now they all laugh, but Hector is serious.

"I want you to know what it's like to ride in the chariot before I leave. I'd hoped for time to train the mare first, but the Lady says otherwise."

"The oracle," Selena corrects.

"Of course, the oracle," Hector nods. "Whoever decreed it, I'm leaving earlier than I hoped. We'll have to do the best we can today."

Awkwardly, Clio climbs in and places her crutch into a strap at the side of the seat, where it stands like a warrior's spear. Her legs sit comfortably on their platform. All the time he's been building it, Clio has never quite believed in this chariot—now she's as excited as Matti.

Hector steps back between the poles, holding them as if he was one of the carrier twins with their tray. The poles are long and awkward when towed by a man instead of a horse; the chariot's left wheel hits a bench full of drying pots. A tall urn smashes onto the floor.

"Goddess leaping!" Selena swears. She's not smiling now.

Matti, shocked, picks up the sharp shards.

"Sorry!" Hector calls, and they escape out to the street.

Dogs rush at the wheels; small children skitter behind them. The weaver's one-footed son rushes behind as if he's going to toss his crutch in and climb aboard too.

"I thought you were off to sea, Troy-man!" the stone vase maker calls. "You've turned into an ox instead!"

"Not an ox," Clio's father protests, and neighs until his friend agrees, "A horse! You've turned into a horse."

Hector prances on out the gate, grinning at the surprised guards. For a moment Clio feels like the Lady being carried through the streets on her palanquin chair. She's not sure if she wants everyone to see her or wants to be invisible.

They turn onto the river road. Two girls hurry ahead with their washing; mothers and children are collecting spring greens on the hills, and as they turn onto the valley path they can see Petros or his brother with the goats. No one is close enough to laugh or mock; Hector is saving his breath for pulling and has stopped neighing or even talking. For the first time Clio settles enough to feel the movement of her body on the woven seat; she can imagine the touch of the reins in her hands.

For just a moment, she can imagine the freedom.

Her father pulls her all the way to the herders' hut. The goats are grazing peacefully farther down the hill while Petros practices with his rope sling, shooting stones at a feathery-leafed tamarisk tree.

Slings look easy when herders use them. The rope whirls, blurring with speed until suddenly one end whips free and the rock flies, fast and lethal as an eagle. Petros and his brother practice whenever they're bored.

His brother can sling a stone farther but Petros could bring down a fleeing hare for dinner every night if he wanted. He's nearly as accurate as their older sister, who's given up practicing in favor of making baskets and soft hide blankets now that her belly is round with a babe.

It wasn't till Clio tried slinging that she realized how difficult it was. Petros had tried to teach her when he first started looking after the horses, but he can't remember when he couldn't do it; he says goatherds grow into it like walking. He showed her how to hold the loop of rope, and how to whirl it, but he couldn't explain how to know just when to let it go. Her rocks thumped to the ground in front of her, wildly off to the side, and even behind. She'd nearly given up even before her fall, and has never tried since.

The last stone hits the target with a *thwack*. Petros loops the rope across his shoulders and comes to greet them. Clio thinks he's going to laugh, but his whistle is pure admiration.

"This is what you've been building!"

Hector nods, lowering the poles and grimacing a little as he rolls his shoulders to relax them. Clio's footrest lowers nearly to the ground; she grabs her crutch and steps out. Her father looks at her, a question on his face.

She doesn't know what to say. For that moment as they turned onto the path she believed in it all; could see herself driving freely where she used to ride—but now she doesn't know whether she'll ever be able to hitch Gray Girl to the chariot herself, let alone train her to pull it. Their bond is from the years that she was on the mare's back, messages passing from legs and hands straight to skin. How can they communicate when they're separated by long wooden poles?

It's impossible. Gray Girl is too used to being ridden. *Maybe we should wait for Fleet Foot to grow up,* she thinks, *or even Fouli—start getting him used to walking between poles while he's still young.*

The horses come up before she can answer. Colti and Fleet Foot pretend to be afraid of the chariot, shying and darting back, though the filly accepts the handful of greens Clio offers. Gray Girl sniffs at it curiously, mouthing the poles as if that's the best way to decide what they are. Fouli stays close to her heels.

Hector, who'd been so irreligious about the oracle that Clio had seen her mother flash the sign against evil, stands with his hand on his heart as he watches the mare. Clio feels a flash of fear as he takes out his small bronze knife, but he simply cuts a lock of Gray Girl's mane and asks to do the same to her. Mingling the horse's coarse gray hairs with his daughter's fine black ones, he calls on the Great Mother and the god of horses.

He pulls the twisted hair bundle in half and hands one part to Clio. "Offer it to the goddess."

She places it on a flat stone outside the entrance to the herders' pen. Traces of blood are on the stone; it's been used for offerings before.

"With this chariot and horse, I will honor and serve the Great Mother," Clio says.

Why did I say that? How can I serve the goddess with a chariot?

Her father holds the other bunch high, speaking to the god of horses in his own tongue, and lets it fly in a sudden gust of wind.

Gray Girl grazes as if this is nothing to do with her. Fouli begins to nurse, and Colti and Fleet Foot wander farther away. Hector brings the harness out from the hut and watches Clio put it on the mare. They've done this so often now that Gray Girl and Clio are both familiar with it, but her father has never studied and checked so carefully before.

He maneuvers the chariot until the mare is between the poles, and connects the harness. Gray Girl steps anxiously as she feels the unfamiliar pressure.

Clio breathes into her nostrils and the mare settles. Maybe because Clio is also stroking between her ears, another of her favorite places.

"Now," says Hector, coming quietly up beside her, "I'll walk by her head, but you'll take the reins."

"From the chariot?"

He nods. "It'll be too light without you in it. Better for her to feel the proper weight."

So though her father is at Gray Girl's head, the horse is pulling and Clio is driving. They take the track back to the river road, following it down to the water's edge and turning at the bridge where women are pounding laundry on the rocks.

"I'll have one of those!" an older woman calls. "That would do nicely to carry these linens!"

"Everyone should have one," Hector agrees happily.

He catches Clio's eye. Even though it's only powerless palace servants—someone shares their vision.

Fouli startles as the women start slapping the wet linen against the rocks. Gray Girl snorts and whickers to him, sidling in the traces. Clio calls out soothingly, ignoring the fears running through her own mind: *I feel so helpless; too far away to stroke her shoulder or calm her through my legs.*

Hector reaches for the bridle and Gray Girl settles. "Don't forget it's the first time you've tried it," he says, dropping back as soon as the horse is calm. "Go on talking to her—she'll soon learn to feel you through the reins as she listens. She's known your voice all her life."

"Clever girl," Clio croons. "What a good job you're doing!"

With Fouli trotting at the mare's shoulder, they head back up the path to the herder's hut. Hector doesn't need to touch the bridle again. Clio breathes a sigh of relief.

It's real, she thinks, *We're really doing it!*

And for just a moment, before Fouli panicked, she had looked over the bridge to the westward road, and thought that they could go anywhere.

Mika has been coming to watch the horses nearly every day, and has studied what the girl and her father do. They offer handfuls of greens and rub behind the horses' ears to greet them; the gray mare lowers her muzzle to the girl's mouth, as if they are sharing the same breath. Sometimes they fasten leather straps around the horses' heads—even on the younger, light brown horse, although they never do anything with her except lead her, for no reason that Mika can see. She's watched them walk behind the gray mare—a long way behind, more than far enough to be out of the way of her back legs—and guide her with the long leather straps attached to the head harness.

But she's never seen anything like this. The gray mare, with the man at her side, is walking down the river path. Behind her is a strange lightweight cart, and in the cart is the girl. The cart is attached to the horse with a harness over its back and chest, but the girl and the horse are attached by those long reins. Suddenly Mika understands why they've been practicing walking behind the mare.

She's a lucky girl after all. Mika hasn't met enough girls her age to ever be truly jealous—and if she'd been jealous of Clio when she first saw her, that quickly changed when she'd watched her using the crutch. But with this cart, the girl's limp no longer matters. She is freer than anyone Mika has ever seen.

The magic stops when the chariot returns to the herder's hut. Out of it, the girl hobbles again. The gray mare is rubbed with dry grass, the cart dragged into a small pen inside the goat enclosure and propped up straight against the hut—even Mika knows that it has to be kept away from the goats, because goats will eat anything.

Before they leave, the man whistles the big black colt, rewards him with a handful of grass, and slips a simple bridle over his head. Unlike the mare's bridle, this one has short reins that the man gathers in one hand before sliding gently onto the horse's back. She's seen him do that before, but this is the first time he's stayed on so long, guiding the horse right around the outside of the enclosure.

Now Mika truly is jealous. She has never wanted anything so badly in her life.

CHAPTER 5
FEASTS AND FAREWELLS

The ships will be farewelled
    at dawn with rites and sacrifice
    demanding blessings from the gods,
    but tonight is for family,
    aunts, uncles, and cousins
    from all through the town.
Hector's clothes are packed—
    spare cloak, tunic,
    and clean white kilt;
    dagger sharpened—
    rubbing, rasping along the whetstone—
    he runs it down his left arm,
    shaving the hairs to test the blade;
    Selena shudders as she always does.
    The same for the small bronze razor—
    he shaves his face clean,

Matti's head too —
packs whetstone and razor,
arrows and hunting bow;
his dagger to be worn with his sailor's kilt
for tomorrow's leaving.
Walking together through the town:
Hector, Selena, Matti,
Clio and her crutch,
carrying wine and gifts for the feast —
and the clay priestess
to preside over all.
Cousin Miso, son of Doulos the captain,
returns from the hills
a year-old ram slung across his shoulders
so they can offer blood to Great Mother
smoke and bones to the god of the sea
and feast on the meat.
Aunt Hella's house
is close to the palace —
she thinks she is almost priest-folk,
as if weaving is dearer to the goddess
than pots —
though the truth is, says Selena
her wealth comes through
Doulos's trading ship —
Leira's family, not hers.
The real truth is
Clio's Mama does not like Hella
because Aunt Hella pities her
for having only one living daughter —

one who is not good at her trade—
and only one grandchild, a boy,
while Aunt Hella has four daughters,
three sons,
and more grandchildren than she can remember.
Doulos holds the ram
above the killing rock at the door
Hella slices her sharp bronze knife
across the woolly throat
as if she were the Lady herself,
while one of her daughters
catches the blood in a bowl.
But when the ram has been turned to meat
threaded on skewers
roasting over the brazier flames,
Clio doesn't care that it's Hella's sheep
or that she's still sick with wishing
something would change so Hector could
stay—
because her mouth waters like a dog's
at the smell
And if the smoke tastes as good to the gods
as it does to her,
all will be well.
They bring the feast cups
made for the night
with the same care as a palace feast
and the wine and water are mixed
in a swallow-painted ewer
that was Grandmother Leira's.

Clio shows Matti
　　how to tip wine from his cup
　　for the Great Mother to drink
　　but this is his first time
　　to be awake at a feast
　　and all that he wants
　　is to smash his cup at the end.
So when Clio tells him,
　　"Dada leaves tomorrow
　　for a long time—
　　two moons, or even three."
"Can we go to the ship to wave bye bye?"
　　asks Matti—
　　as if waving is the only thing that matters
　　and Clio says yes,
　　pushing down her rage
　　because Matti is too young to understand—
　　and no one else seems to care
　　that if the goddess rejects the statue
　　this may be the last time
　　Clio will see her father.
But now Aunt Hella is chanting,
　　cousins are clapping,
　　the dancing beginning,
　　and she pushes rage down
　　to offer her steps as best she can.
Shoulder to shoulder, arms firm around waists—
　　no need for a crutch in this circling family—
　　whirling, stamping, chanting,
　　offering joy to delight the goddess.

"Never have people worshiped as we do!"
their steps proclaim,
"Keep us safe and we will offer
this love to you over and over again."
And with each stamp, each twirl and skip,
    Clio forgets the leg that drags;
    her heart swings higher,
    light as Matti's, full of hope,
    shedding gloom and anger
    till her voice breaks free
    to sing with her mother and aunts
    resting only
    for more drink and meat.
Though when the feasting is done
    and chins mutton-juice greasy
    the last praise has been danced,
    the wine drained,
    and empty cups dashed in the fire—
    their sacrifice a final gift
    to bring good winds and trade at sea,
    peace and plenty at home—
    Matti's cheer is the loudest,
    as everyone older
    celebrates through unshed tears.
Selena links arms with Hector,
    pressing close to his side—
    the broken urn forgiven—
    and Clio cuddles Matti,
    not caring how he squirms and wriggles
    but wishing he could always stay

outside the world of fear,
locked in the wonder of smashing cups
and waving ships bye bye.

At dawn they crowd to the palace courtyard to see the Lady call the sun. Selena yearns for all the family to be there together, but it's too long for the statue to be left alone and she can't carry it with her for fear of being jostled in the bustling courtyard. Clio has never seen her look so torn. Aunt Fotia, Selena's older sister, has been sharing the vigil with them, but her eldest grandson is sailing with Uncle Doulos for the first time, so she's not going to stay away from the ceremonies.

Besides, Fotia and her family moved out of the house a long time ago, when Hector moved in. It's Selena's family who's lived and worked here with Grandmother Leira—the responsibility of the vigil is theirs.

In the end they compromise. Clio will go to see the sun rise and Selena will farewell the ship.

Not fair! thinks Clio. *Every year, for as long as I can remember, I've watched the start of the sailing season rites and waved to Dada till the ship is no more than a dot on the waves.*

So waving bye bye is more important than the vigil for the clay priestess? asks an irritating voice in her head. Clio ignores it.

Hector swings Matti to his shoulders and they follow the cobblestone road through the town to the palace—and even though it was Mama who'd decided, it seems wrong to go without her.

If Grandmother Leira was still alive, she could have stayed behind with the statue! She hardly ever went to the dawn ceremony anymore.

It's a small part of wishing that her grandmother was still in this life. She was old and weak, but the world was safer when she was here. Now it's as if the house has lost its roof—the family is open to the sky and whatever the gods rain on them.

On her wooden stage in the dim light of the courtyard, with the east mountain looming darker behind her, the Lady begins to sing. Slowly, slowly, she calls the sun up from behind the mountain into the pale sky. Blinding the audience, streaking the sky with pink and gold, the miracle of sunrise happens again.

Clio feels the warmth of her father's hand on her shoulder. His other hand is firmly on Matti's left ankle, in case he decides to jump in the middle of the ritual. He's done it before.

The last notes of the song die away. The townfolk are still blinking in the sun's dazzle, and the Lady waits a moment until they can see her standing on her stage, the chief beside her. She is wearing the ceremonial dress Grandmother Leira copied for the statue: the flounced skirt and sacred apron, her snake-decorated bodice open to the waist, and the tall cone of hat that makes her taller than any man. White paint makes her face a mask; her eyes are huge and dark, and her lips red. Her voice is firm and strong. When she's been consulting the oracle, her voice is higher, stranger, almost sleepy; sometimes the power of the gods is so great she has trouble standing. But today this is the voice of a leader.

"Never before have the ships sailed so early in the year."

Everyone knows that! thinks Clio.

"The goddess decreed that in this time of danger, our ships should begin their trading as early as possible, to return with goods and wealth for the coming year."

Hector murmurs, "It's true. The first ships catch the best trade."

"Our town is strong. We have brave men and women here to defend our homes if we need to, and by leaving now, our sailors will sooner be home with us again, perhaps in no more than two moons."

Clio's father's hand tightens on her shoulder in a promise.

Now the Lady in her palanquin chair, the chief and the guards lead the way, Uncle Doulos and the other ship's captain close behind them with their families at their sides. Hector should be up at the front too, but he lingers so that they are nearly at the end.

Delia waves from across the crowd, but for once Clio doesn't want to be with her friend. She waves back and stays with her Dada.

Selena hadn't said exactly when they should change places, so Clio keeps on walking with Hector, out the gate and down the road to the pier where the ships wait on the beach. Uncle Doulos is standing by his ship already. It's very old because it was his grandfather's—Leira's father's—ship, but it's been freshly painted and the swallow on the side shines bright behind the long shaft of the bowsprit.

Aunt Hella and the rest of Uncle Doulos's family surround him in a circle of farewell hugs. It's well past time for Clio to say good-bye. Her father lifts Matti from his shoulders and hugs him hard, then holds Clio so close she could almost suffocate. She knows she needs to run home so her mother can say her own good-bye, but is glad he doesn't tell her to leave.

"Go with the goddess," he says, choking on the words and adding quickly, "and give me news of the horses when I return." Because the looming spring festival means that "go with the goddess" suddenly sounds like a curse rather than a blessing.

One of the guards lays a goat on the offering stone in front of the pier; another is carrying a jug of wine. Priestesses chant and clap; the chief raises his bronze ax to glint in the sun while the Lady holds a fine blood-catching bowl—even from here Clio can see the swallow that says it comes from Grandmother Leira's studio. She has to run now.

She turns and pushes her way through the crowd, shoving past shocked faces and jostling bodies all trying to get closer to the ships, towing little Matti behind her.

What if I've left it too late for Mama to say good-bye! "You go to the dawn ceremony," Selena had said, "then come home so I can go to the ship-leaving."

Clio hadn't meant to stay for both; it just happened, she tells herself—though she doesn't quite believe her own lie.

She's just off the beach, before the first curve on the road to town, when she sees her mother running toward her.

"Go!" Selena shouts, pointing toward home, and scooping Matti up in her arms, keeps running toward the beach.

"They haven't done the sacrifice yet!" Clio calls back, hoping she's telling the truth. Even if the lamb has been killed, there'll be more prayers and chanting before its blood and the wine are poured over the ships' bowsprits. With each splash of spray washing over the bow, the sea gods will taste the sacrifice and be reminded that if they want more offerings like it, they need to bring these sailors safely home.

Sometimes Clio thinks the gods are like horses: you never know what they're going to do, but the more treats you offer them, the more likely they are to care for you.

Did I just compare the gods to horses? But even as she makes the sign against evil, she hears another voice in her head: her grandmother, laughing. "The world is crazy," Leira used to say, "and all we can do is humor the gods and laugh."

Which was never any help but makes Clio feel better as she swings herself through the town gates and home, as fast as her crutch will carry her.

The room is dark, because the window's in the west

and not much sunlight is coming in yet, but she can see the shape of the statue, safe on the shrine in the corner. She stands before it with her hand on her heart. "It's my fault Mama had to leave you."

"I'm sure it was!" a voice snaps. "You've always been a disrespectful girl, crazy as a goat-kid in spring."

Clio's heart stops. The statue has come to life!

Slowly, slowly, the room comes into focus. The statue doesn't move, but there's another shape on the stool beside the shrine, and now Clio recognizes the cackle: "You thought it was alive! Oh, you foolish child! It's a good thing your grandmother isn't alive to see how witless and wicked you are—'The girl's got a good heart,' she'd always tell me. 'She'll grow up all right.' Hah! She wouldn't have said that if she'd known you'd run away from your vigil. Is it so much to ask? Your grandmother pours her life into this statue, and you can't sit vigil for it!"

Granny Pouli, from the winemakers across the road. No one knows how old she is; maybe even older than Leira was. *Why couldn't the gods have taken her instead?*

Clio flicks her fingers against evil again. Some days she thinks she should just make the sign all day long, one hand constantly flicking against whatever her mind comes up with next.

"Your mother asked me to come in when you didn't come back. Though why your father didn't send you home earlier—but he's foreign, no idea of how things should be done."

"It's not my father's fault! I just wanted to say good-bye."

"And you thought your mother didn't?"

There's no answer for that. "I'm back now," Clio says sullenly, placing her hand on her heart again. "Thank you for watching in my place."

Her belly is churning with anger and guilt, but as she holds the sign and watches the old woman return it, she starts to settle. Granny Pouli is not a potter and she's not family, but she's been her grandmother's neighbor since Leira was married and started her own workshop. Neighbor-cousin, Clio's grandmother had called her, because you don't have to like all your cousins, but they're still family.

"Thank you," she says again. This time she means it.

Fear hovers at the edges of minds;
    bright and elusive as Great Mother's dragonflies
    and as hard to ignore.
    Sharpening tempers and words,
    forming demon-dreams
    to descend in dark nights.
Even Matti,
    not yet four summers old
    is trapped in night horrors
    he's too young to understand—
    and rage fills her,
    flaring like oil splashed on a torch
    to think that harm could come to him.

Because when Matti winds arms
    around her neck
    and legs round her waist
    he is solid and warm
    as a heated stone on a winter night.
    His laugh shows small white teeth
    and it brightens the darkest room
    or mood
    just to see him
    squatting on the workshop floor,
    gathering pinches of fallen clay
    to knead and squeeze,
    shape and pat—
    he will be, she thinks,
    a master crafter like Selena—
    so that if she should ever
    have a child of her own
    she could not love it
    more than him.
Clio thinks that if she knew
    Matti would grow strong and safe
    from warriors or famine
    she could almost accept
    what the Great Mother demands.
    But the goddess,
    Grandmother Leira once said,
    takes all we can give
    and doesn't always give back.
So sometimes, even when she sits
    with the small painted priestess—

a face that mirrors her own,
though stronger, fiercer,
than she thinks she could be—
doubt wiggles in.
And when she remembers the ship
with its warriors in training
cold fear settles like a stone in her belly—
for herself, for Matti,
her mama, and family
her heart-friend Delia,
for every stone of this seagazing town,
and her horses out on the hills.
The only way she can chase
that sickening fear
is to punch the clay
harder than it needs,
or to sing high and loud
till her throat is raw.
The pottery floor
has always hummed with song,
to help the wheel call the clay into life,
but now fear creeps
into any spot of silence
and the song's first job
is to drive it out.
But for Clio the best of all
is hurrying to the hills,
whistling the horses
to gallop toward her,
thundering beauty,

whispering soft noses over her face
till she knows the world
has nothing to fear.

While his sister secretly watches the horses, the octopus
fisher spies on the town. From a shrubby thicket at
the edge of the barley field, he sees the ships depart,
the oars flashing in unison—though not as strictly and
perfectly as he's seen on the black ships wintering near
Tarmara. Halfway across the bay, the oars are shipped
and the big square sail raised. For a moment Dymos
imagines the freedom of traveling with the wind to
strange new lands.

But the thought that keeps turning in his mind—
that makes him want to dance with glee—is of how
many men have gone with the ships. The town that
mocked him has never been so defenseless.

The sight of a girl racing across the bridge jolts him
from his revenge fantasies. She's moving fast, crouching
low to keep hidden—but stiffly, as if she's been beaten.
It's his sister.

His rage flares again. He races out from behind the
shrub to grab her by the arm, dragging her the rest of
the way across the bridge.

Mika gasps in fear. She hadn't seen him at all.

"Where have you been? Who hit you?"

"I fell out of a tree."

It could almost be true—her tunic is dusty as if
she's landed hard on her bottom, but he can't think
of any reason she should be climbing a tree, especially

on this side of the river. She hadn't even been brave enough to cross the bridge with him that miserable feast day. She's up to something—and he'll get it out of her eventually.

In spite of herself, Mika glances back across the river. Her brother follows her gaze to see three horses and a foal grazing at the bottom of a hill, watched over by a goatherd. For the first time this moon, Dymos smiles.

Spring has arrived. The sun had already started growing hotter in the days before the ships sailed, bringing the first bright flowers and wild greens. Praise the goddess, thinks Clio, this morning is as misty as a winter's day and the plants on the freshly green hills will be growing strong. Children and old people—anyone not working or on wall-building duty—head out with baskets to pluck salad greens: chicory, chervil, mallow and dandelion, and the fresh shoots of wild asparagus before they turn to thistles.

Clio can't remember if the first day after Dada leaves is always like this, she and her mother edging around each other as if they have to find a new way to be a family again. One moment Selena wants to keep her daughter close by her side as if she were as young as Matti—and the next moment snaps as if the sight of Clio makes her angrier than she can bear. But she knows that the horses must be checked and when Clio has finished as many cups as can be spread in the sun to dry, Selena says she should go.

"Take a basket for greens," she adds, grumbly again after hugging Clio so tight she can't breathe. "Might as well do something useful while you're out there."

Clio takes a basket but collecting salad is not what she's thinking of. It's two days since she drove the chariot for the first time. It feels like a moon cycle ago and she's afraid that if she doesn't try soon she won't ever be brave enough again.

The horses come quickly to her whistle. Petros and the goats are farther up the hill; she's glad that she isn't completely alone—and even happier that her friend isn't close enough to see her nervousness. She's worried that she won't be able to put the harness on and attach the chariot by herself, even though she'd done it in front of Hector; she's very afraid that she won't be able to control Gray Girl if she startles—and most of all, she's terrified of breaking the chariot.

But she's bridled the mare countless times over the years and harnessing is not so different. By the time she's double-checked that the traces are attached she's starting to feel calmer. The scariest moment is placing her crutch in its strap with her left hand, holding the reins firmly in her right and gripping the chariot side rail at the same time so she doesn't yank them as she backs into the seat.

She's done it! Gray Girl is still standing attentively, waiting to see what Clio wants—and what Clio wants is exactly this: to be sitting in her chariot, her legs on their support and the reins in her hand, ready to go. Golden as sunshine, a wave of relief washes through her.

They circle the goat enclosure twice; Petros waves his arms in celebration from the hill. Clio pictures driving triumphantly up to see him, but the ground is rough and rocky, so she waves back and takes the smoother path to the river. Fouli stays tight at Gray Girl's side while Fleet Foot and Colti amble behind.

Clio turns in the same spot that she had with Hector. Already it's easier. And again, she sees the bridge and road beckoning with their promise of freedom.

Driving will never be like riding, but she's starting to believe it could work.

The chief has ordered bronze smelting to be stepped up to produce as many daggers and spearheads as possible before the raw materials run out. The metal workers have set up new foundries near the kilns, melting copper and tin together to create the stronger, more valuable metal. Boys pump the great hide bellows, flaming the fires into heat as intense as the sun. Igor the Bronze's daughter Ada takes a turn pumping when she's not forging.

Delia's mother has been commanded to make terracotta pipes that funnel the hot air from the bellows to the fires. "Our pots are just as fine as yours!" Delia snaps. "Anyone could make bellows pipes!"

"No one's making pots for trade now the ships are gone," Clio points out. "We're only making feast cups—any workshop could definitely make those. The pipes are probably the most important thing a potter can make right now."

She knows that Delia is angry about more than making pipes. In these last few days something has changed between them and Clio's not sure what it is—until finally, at the end of a shared lunch of spring greens and yogurt from Petros's goats, Delia snaps, "If you'd just put your own pots in the kiln that morning the oracle would never have spoken! Didn't you realize the goddess would be angry you abandoned her figures? Do you think she'll accept another figurine from your workshop, no matter how beautiful it is?"

What makes it worse is that it's exactly what Clio's been thinking, and what she's sure her mother believes, though Mama's never quite said so. But Delia...Delia's her friend, the one who sticks by her no matter what she's done or said.

But if Grandmother Leira has died for nothing, breathing life into a statue the goddess won't accept, Clio thinks, *I'm the one who will pay. I don't see why Delia is so angry.*

She's too restless to sleep at siesta. "Go," says her mother. "It's nothing to the Palace whether you rest or visit your horses."

Gray Girl and Fleet Foot come to her whistle, as hungry for the few greens Clio's picked as if they hadn't been grazing on the same thing all night. Fleet Foot snatches hers, but Gray Girl's soft dark lips tickle the girl's palms, and her snort when she's finished tickles even more. Fouli nibbles cautiously, still finding it strange to eat from a hand.

Colti doesn't appear; he often lags behind, especially now the fields are lush. Clio whistles again.

Petros is facing the other way up the hill, practicing slinging stones. His old dog is sleeping against the wall, too deaf to hear Clio coming; the young dog is out of sight. Clio waves but Petros doesn't see her. He goes on pelting a small tree so furiously she's surprised it hasn't broken.

Not Petros too! thinks Clio. Because he must know she's here by now; the goats are bleating and skittering as if they've never seen her before.

They're afraid.

And that makes her afraid, though she doesn't know what of.

Finally Petros coils his sling and comes toward her. His eyes are red and his face swollen. The old dog gets up and limps over to him, licking his hand for comfort.

The young dog still isn't in sight. Neither is Colti.

"Wild dogs," Petros says at last. "They came in last night. The goats were in the pen, but the horses were in the field. I grabbed a branch from the fire, and the dog and I went out."

Clio's heart freezes. "Colti?" she asks, desperately looking around.

"I haven't seen him this morning," says Petros. "The dogs scattered the horses then went after your little Fouli. The mare attacked them—and my dog went to help. The wild ones killed him."

He looks so broken she wants to hug him as she would Matti—but Petros is a boy of her own age, an almost-man; they are too old and too young to hug each other, in this in-between time.

But a hand on his arm, surely that's not forbidden. His eyes fill with tears; he puts his own hand on hers and squeezes it.

"He was a good dog," he says, his voice choking.

"And I thank him for saving Fouli."

"I had my sling—but it was too dark, I couldn't use it in case I hit my own dog or the horses. I think I got one when they were running away, but it was too late."

"It's one that won't come back." She knows it's not much comfort.

He nods, letting her hand go. "I've searched for Colti down to the river and over this hill, but the flock has been so restless I couldn't go farther."

"I'll harness Gray Girl."

For just a moment she feels stronger than she ever has, a strange energy running through her like a gold thread through the black fear. She knows she can do what she must.

I'm making the wheels strong as a war chariot, Dada said, *so you can go where you need on the hills.*

Selena always says that a cart or chariot is useless because there isn't any smooth ground where it's safe to go. Hector says the raiders will leave one day and when they do, he'll take the horses to deliver his wife's beautiful pots all the way to Tarmara.

It's probably not true—even Hector admits that a

horse can't pull as much as an ox, so if it doesn't matter how fast they get there, goods will always be taken by oxcart. That's why most townfolk argue that horses aren't as useful as goats. "They carry a little more but eat ten times as much," Selena likes to say.

But, like the folk of Hector's home country, the raiders love horses. Sometimes when the horses don't come to Clio's first whistle, she's afraid they might have wandered far enough for the raiders to see them. Afraid they might be captured and used for war against their own people.

Sometimes her head feels ready to burst with all the bad things that might happen—but now she's stroking Gray Girl, checking that the girth and chest straps are on tight and straight and that she's connected the chariot properly. She doesn't want the mare to sense her anxiety, and she mustn't rush and make a mistake in harnessing, but doing it this slowly feels like pushing through mud. It seems a long time before she places her crutch in its strap and slides into the chariot.

"Find Colti," she says, clucking her tongue and lifting the reins.

Gray Girl moves strongly across the hill, Fouli at her heels and Fleet Foot trotting beside. The day is warm and the scent of thyme is strong when one of them steps on it, bees flitting away as they pass.

Clio remembers riding one long-ago day when a bee stung the mare's tender flank. Gray Girl bucked, throwing Clio hard onto her bottom—if she'd had a tail it would have been broken. It stung like a scorpion bite for three days and then healed, not even leaving her with an omen of what would happen a year later.

What will happen if she shies while she's pulling the chariot? I don't know if I could control her...I wish I'd had longer to learn from Dada. All I know is that I don't want to break the chariot or hurt my mare. And if I have less than two moons left above the earth, I don't want to live them in pain.

How did that demon-dream thought sneak into this day? Of course the goddess will accept the statue!

"We mean you no harm, bees," she calls. "Let us pass and make your honey in peace."

A little way farther up the hill, she spots Colti. Relief melts through her—she didn't know she'd been so afraid he was dead until now she's seen him alive. Happily grazing on the wrong side of the river.

Clio whistles; Gray Girl whickers. Fouli looks up alarmed and trots to her side; Colti lifts his head but doesn't move. Fleet Foot neighs and the colt ignores her too.

"Let's go, Gray Girl," says Clio, lifting the reins.

The mare doesn't need to be told. She likes her companions around her; neighing again, she follows the track winding toward the river.

Clio pulls her up at the top of the gully path. It's too narrow for the chariot—but she doesn't need to go down it to see that the thorn barricade has been pulled away.

Could Colti have done that, even in his terror?

Maybe. Maybe the goats started it and Petros didn't notice.

But goats would eat it, not pull it aside. Colti would have trampled it. Only people could pull it away.

What if they weren't wild dogs? What if they were a thief and his dogs?

Don't be ridiculous! A thief from where? Everyone knows the horses are ours.

However it happened, she can't imagine how frightened the colt must have been, scrambling up that steep bank on the other side in the dark.

But what matters now is getting him back. And Clio can't go through the river in the chariot—she'll have to cross the bridge.

Gray Girl doesn't understand about chariots and rough river beds. She is trumpeting for Colti, and it's all Clio can do to hold her back from plunging into the water. It's the first time they've argued since she's been driving—and if Gray Girl wins, they could lose the colt as well as the chariot.

"Stay calm", her father would say. "Stay calm," Clio says to herself.

But fear and frustration meld like copper and tin into bronze, and a scream of rage bursts out. "Goddess leaping, Gray Girl! Just do what I tell you!"

Gray Girl finally turns obediently up to the track that leads to the river road. Clio feels sick with shame and relief.

It's afternoon now; the washers have finished for the day. No one's in sight as Gray Girl steps onto the bridge. They've never crossed it before, even when Clio was riding. The mare's hooves ring on the stone; the chariot's wooden wheels creak and rattle.

Gray Girl flattens her ears and tosses her head in protest. Fouli dances on the edge, stepping onto the bridge and darting backwards. Fleet Foot doesn't even try to cross it and bolts back to the entrance to the valley, whinnying anxiously.

The country on this side of the river is not so well tended. There are flocks of goats and sheep on the hills and tracks down to the river, but between the tracks the banks are tangled and shrubby. Clio's skin prickles as she leaves her familiar world.

Gray Girl turns her head to look back over the bridge and trumpets to Fouli, her tone as sharp as Clio's own mother's would be. *Come now!* she's saying—and he does.

She takes a moment to sniff the foal while he noses for comfort milk.

"You're not nervous of the chariot when you want a drink, are you?" Clio teases him, imagining how the story would make Dada smile.

Suddenly, she hears a neigh from the riverside brush. Gray Girl whickers back and Colti appears.

He's not alone. A girl is with him.

She's younger than Clio, ten summers or eleven at most, dressed in a short, frayed tunic and carrying a basket of greens. The colt noses at it, snatching leaves, and the girl looks as pleased as if he'd bowed down to worship her.

Clio hears Dada's voice in her ear: *Don't let strangers feed your horses—they should be loyal only to you.*

"Keep away from that horse!" she shouts, and the girl jumps. She's been so intent on Colti that she hasn't seen Clio.

"Why?" Her voice is trembling but defiant. "I can pick more greens."

"He doesn't know you—he might bite."

The girl looks disbelieving and doesn't move away. Clio whistles, but Colti doesn't believe that she's got greens, or that Gray Girl would let him have them if she did. He's right on both points.

But while the girl is still staring at Clio, the colt snatches her basket, crunching the reeds before tossing the whole thing away with a flick of his head.

"My basket!"

Clio almost says, "I warned you!" but the girl's crying. Besides, she doesn't have any time to waste in talking—she needs to find a wide enough space on the road to turn the horse and chariot, and get all the horses back to her side of the river.

She's urging Gray Girl forward when she sees the basket dangling from a branch, well out of the girl's reach. Clio grabs her crutch from its strap, and hooks the basket down.

The colt has ripped the side out; the girl will need to make a new one. *Her mother won't be pleased*, thinks Clio.

She tosses her the ruined basket, which makes Gray Girl snort and sidle. "Calm, girl," Clio soothes, trying to keep the reins firm without jerking. It works. It's the first time she's communicated more than *Stop!* or *Turn here!* with the reins.

The girl's eyes are as wide with wonder as if Clio had walked across the sea. "How do you do that?" she breathes.

"I've been riding her since I was a baby." Clio skips quickly over any questions about whether she can ride now. "She does what I say."

"Gods' teeth!" Hector would have said. "Are you asking for the horse to bolt?"

Clio quickly makes another sign against evil and hopes the gods weren't listening. But having someone look at her like that was like sunshine on a winter day after all the cold rainy looks from Delia. She wants to bask in that warmth like a lizard on a rock.

"What's your name?"

"Mika, from the village of fishers." The girl gestures to the other side of the point, far from the town's own fisher village. That's why Clio's never seen her before.

She relents. This girl is no danger. "You can touch my horse, Mika—with your hand flat, gently on her shoulder."

Tentative as a wild animal herself, the girl comes close. Gray Girl sidles at the fishy smell, but Clio speaks to her with reins and voice till the mare settles. Mika strokes gently, her face shining. Gently, and surprisingly confidently.

It's me she's scared of, Clio thinks, not the horses. But how could a child of a fishing settlement know horses?

"Why do you come all this way just to gather a basket of greens?"

"It's not so far if you follow the goat path between the hills to the river," Mika says, blushing a liar's red. "And my brother said he'd seen horses on the other side. I wanted to see too."

Clio knows she'd go a long way to see horses like this—but it doesn't make sense for a fisher girl.

"Is this your life?" Mika asks, before Clio can frame her next question. "Doesn't a horse herder have to stay with them all the time?"

"What do you mean?" Clio demands. "How do you know I'm not with the horses all the time?"

Mika's blush deepens further. She points to Colti. "I saw this one when I came this morning and you've only started looking for him now. If I had a horse like this I'd look after him all the time."

Anger burns Clio's face as hot as Mika's. "The horses were attacked in the night by wild dogs—or maybe thieves!"

"Thieves!" Mika repeats, the blood draining from her face. "No! He wouldn't!"

"Who wouldn't?"

"No one! I meant no one would steal the horses!" Mika turns to stroke Colti, the same way Clio would stroke Gray Girl for comfort—*as if she knows him*, thinks Clio. *Or as if she doesn't want to meet my eye.*

"I said keep away from that one!" She shouts, louder than she meant to. Fouli startles, kicking out with both hind legs and bumping Mika. The girl throws her arms up to stop herself from falling and hits the mare's sensitive nose. Gray Girl rears; the chariot tips; Clio's crutch slides out to the ground and Clio nearly does too.

Clio throws her weight forward, calming the mare with her voice, but by the time she settles, Colti is galloping down the riverbank.

And now Mika, who caused it all, is handing her the crutch. "I thought you said the horses do what you want."

"Not when someone startles them!"

Clio catches her breath enough to whistle. She can't take the chariot down that rough riverbank—she'll have to trust that he'll come.

Mika is already running down a narrow goat track through the bushes. After a moment she's disappeared.

Is she so afraid of me that she's running away?

She can't worry about this strange girl. She whistles again.

Gray Girl's ears flick and she turns to look at Clio. "Why aren't we moving?" her big eyes say. She's always surprised when something happens from her rearing, as if it's nothing to do with her.

Colti will come back eventually, Clio's sure of it. If she can't follow him, the next best thing will be to turn the chariot around so Gray Girl's ready to lead him back across the bridge.

The road widens on the flatter ground ahead; Clio clucks for Gray Girl to move on and they turn. It's not as smooth as the day before and she's happy that the girl isn't here to watch.

Why do I care what she thinks? Why did I waste all that time talking to her? And what if Colti doesn't come back... What if she's stealing him?

If she was on Gray Girl's back she'd follow them—but in her chariot, her wonderful chariot, Clio is helpless. She brushes away angry tears, her mind spinning frantically, more panicked with every breath.

Gray Girl whickers—and Colti appears, coming back up the river bank the way he'd gone.

Mika is right behind him, out of breath and triumphant. "I took a shortcut and herded him back."

Clio's impressed in spite of herself. "Thank you."

She whistles again, more softly this time, and Colti steps toward them, calmly snatching at grasses along his way.

Clio's expected him to be panicked. She's even more impressed—but still objects when the girl offers him a handful of dandelion leaves.

"Don't feed him!"

"He likes it."

"You can't touch him if I'm not here. It's not safe— he might rear like Gray Girl did and trample you." *Or they all might get to know you and make it easier for you to steal one of them.*

Mika trails behind as they leave. "Will you be here tomorrow?"

"Farther up the river, on the other side," says Clio. "I need to fix the barrier so they don't get out again."

They rattle their way onto the bridge. Fouli crosses

bravely this time. He is tired and staying with his mother is more important than unfamiliar noises.

But the colt hesitates. He wants to follow Gray Girl but whirls back with shock each time his front hoof thumps onto the stone. *How will I get him back if he turns and gallops the wrong way down the road?*

That's just what he's going to do. He gets one front hoof onto the bridge—but as the second one touches, he shoots backwards and whirls to flee.

"Hah!" Mika is there, jumping in front of him, arms waving wildly—and Colti is turning back.

If the bank wasn't so steep and rocky he'd jump into the river, but he has no choice. He bolts across the bridge to join his herd on the path. He forgets his terror the instant he's on the other side, rubbing heads with Fleet Foot and falling into line with her behind the chariot—like Matti hugging Mama after a tantrum about something he knows he can't have.

Clio signs her thanks to Mika.

"I'll help you fix the fence tomorrow!" the other girl shouts.

"In the morning!" calls Clio. She needs help—and how could she say no after Mika bringing Colti back?

Gray Girl trotting for home
    calm as if she's pulled a chariot
    and crossed the bridge every day of her life.
The goats are roaming
    high up to the peak—
    but Petros is watching

down to the river,
hand shading eyes from setting sun.
Clio never knew
he loved the horses
but he runs through the flock
face lighting with joy
to see the cantering colt
home safe.
At the hut,
Clio wearier than she knew,
legs shaking with strain
to stand after so long,
she leans heavy on her crutch,
so that Petros, without a word,
tows the chariot away
while she rubs Gray Girl's sweating shoulders
with tufts of dry grass
and checks no straps have rubbed—
Hector's work is good.
Colti prances, as if to prove
the dog gave his life well
for though his dark coat
is stained with dry sweat,
there's no trace of a wound
or mark of sharp teeth.
Petros thanks the gods
and the spirit of his dog—
but relief that the death was not in vain
doesn't change the truth—
he has no dog to herd.

"I have a pup," he says
    "but not yet weaned—
    he won't be working
    till spring next year.
    This old fellow
    will move the herd if he sees my signs—
    but he doesn't hear,
    or even see well enough
    to find a stray kid without my help."
He doesn't need to say
    what they both know—
    this aging dog was already too old
    when the horses first came
    to live with the goats.
    Gray Girl kicked him once
    and the dog decided
    that horses are not his job.
"With my brother gone to sea
    and my sister near her time
    we need a good dog."
    Though as he speaks
    he strokes the old head
    as if the dog can hear.
    "Or perhaps out in the hills
    there's a herder with a child to spare—
    it might be easier to train
    than a stranger's half-grown dog."
"The gods may have sent us one,"
    says Clio, and tells him of the girl
    herding Colti home.

But Petros spits,
    "A fisher could never learn
    the ways of the flock—
    to see that they're ill
    before they drop,
    to know each doe,
    each buck and kid
    by their call and gait,
    as only a herder can."
Clio tells him
    the girl's face lit like a lamp
    when she stroked the mare;
    that she watches them as if she knows—
    and his face grows darker still.
"This girl, this stranger
    watching your horses
    the very day after
    the dogs attacked
    and the fence was broken.
    What if the dogs were herding
    not to kill
    but to drive the horses across the river
    for the fishers to steal?"
His words would chill Clio less
    if they hadn't already run through her mind—
    her shout of "No!"
    is to those running thoughts:
    "What would a fisher
    ever want with a horse?"

CHAPTER 6
THE THORN FENCE

The chief calls another meeting at sunset. Mama stays home with the statue and Matti. "I should be the one to go," she protests, but she's barely slept since Dada left and is haggard with exhaustion. Clio wins the argument.

Clio has often seen her mother headachy and fatigued, but this is the first time she's had to take the responsibility. Until now, if Hector was away, Grandmother Leira was there, quietly directing anything that she couldn't do herself.

She follows the crowd to the court. When she bumps into Delia at the entrance, the morning's uneasiness dissolves; they stand close together, holding hands against the fear. A sunset meeting hasn't been called since they were babies—this is serious.

"At least it's not another oracle," Delia whispers.

A guard bangs a gong for silence. Clio and Delia squeeze hands.

A messenger has come from a village near Tarmara, the chief proclaims.

He's standing on the palace balcony, the Lady on her throne beside him and the priests behind. The flare of burning torches lights their faces and white kilts, glints off the bronze spear tips of the guards. The audience is a mass of darkness.

"The raiders are readying for war."

Wailing rises from the dark courtyard. The guard beats his gong again.

"This is as we expected," booms the chief. "We do not know when they will come. The oracle said the Great Mother wanted our sailors to leave in good health to return with new wealth. We have done what she said—the ships may be home before an attack comes."

A swell of muttering says that no one believes him. Raiders are not going to wait for another two or three cycles of the moon.

"But our wall rebuilding is too slow. You will now give the wall one day's work in three. When the bellows pipes and feast cups are completed, potters will no longer be exempt. Children of three summers and up will collect stones for slings."

"How do I mind my sheep and work on a wall at the same time?" Cross-Eye the shepherd demands, braver than anyone else. "My children are young and my wife is dead: there's no one to take my place."

"The Great Mother will be pleased," the Lady says calmly, "to add your sheep to the palace flock. Her herders will care for straying animals, or for others where the burden is too great for their owners."

"You'll be fed for your work on the wall," the chief adds, "and you won't have to worry about your flock."

The crowd growls like a dog ready to spring.

"But that makes him a slave!" Clio exclaims to her mother once she's home. Selena nods bitterly.

She agrees that Clio needs to go out early and help Petros rebuild the barrier to the river. This is not the time to have the horses escape.

"Leave with the dawn," Selena adds. "The guards may not remember that the Lady ordered our vigil with the statue."

So they greet the dawn at home, just the three of them. It's a small group without Grandmother Leira and Hector, but if they went to the court, either Selena or Clio would have to stay home, so it would be even worse. They take the statue outside with them so it can hear the Lady's notes echoed in every home where someone is ill, in childbirth, or mourning. Their voices lift and mingle, part of the town, one body serving the Great Mother.

And for these moments, it binds Selena and Clio closer together. Matti too, except that Matti is always close in both their hearts. Sometimes Clio thinks he's the only bridge between them.

Selena pours three cups of ale; Clio brings out cheese and the barley cakes, baked the day before Hector left and getting stale now. Still enough for tomorrow, though, so they don't have to bake today. No more dried figs, and still another six moons or seven before this year's ripen.

Will I be here for the figs?

She offers another small slurp of ale to the goddess, dripping it to the ground in front of the statue. Can the figurine see now, before it's consecrated? Clio thinks so. She hopes so. She faces the statue again with her hand on her heart.

Her mother mirrors the gesture.

Matti swipes the half-eaten barley cake Selena has put down to pray. He's always hungry these days. "Matti!" his grandmother sighs, too tired to scold — then remembers he must be sent out to collect stones. She hugs him as if her heart is breaking.

"You take him to the field," she tells her daughter. "Then check your horses quickly so you can go on making the feast cups with me."

Matti's still a baby! Clio thinks rebelliously. *It's one thing for him to help in the studio, but not to spend a day carrying stones.*

And while he works, she'll be seeing the horses she loves, then throwing simple cups on her potter's wheel as if the coming feast is no different from any other.

She's close to tears as she leads the little boy out through the town gate.

On the side of the road to the sea, a group of small children are gathering around a young boy guard. He holds up a rounded stone as big as an eagle's egg. "Bring me more like this!"

A tiny girl, even younger than Matti, picks up a stone at the boy's feet and presents it proudly.

"You're stupider than the stones!" the boy guard shouts. "That's one I just found!"

The toddler bursts into tears. Her older brother grabs her hand. "We'll find some over here," he says, leading her toward the olive grove. Clio recognizes them—a weaver's children from farther down their street. The boy is barely five summers but has more quiet authority than the one who'll be a leader of guards one day.

She leaves Matti with him. The five year-old is one of his heroes, and as Clio hurries on to the river road, she hears Matti's excited squeal as he finds a perfect stone.

Petros isn't with the herd, and he's not at the river crossing. The goats and the horses are scattered across the hills, while the old dog sits by the empty hut, watching and waiting. He gives a half growl as Clio approaches and looks wary even when she's close enough to recognize.

Anger churns in her stomach like curdled milk. *Why do the gods play these games? Do they sit back and laugh while we scurry around like ants in a kicked-over hill?*

Because now, while Petros is the only one in his family fit to herd and the palace is demanding even more labor, they have one dog too old to work and one too young.

The palace will take any beasts you can't care for!

The threat rings in her mind; chills her blood. Petros's family's goats; her family's horses...*Never!* She thinks. *Never, never, never.*

She has to do all she can in the time she has. To save her horses for as long as she can, from wild dogs, thieves, raiders, and the palace.

Petros would never desert the flock unless he had no choice. He must have been called to work on the wall. His father died last year; his brother is on the ship with Hector. If his sister's baby is coming today, their mother will be with her.

Clio will have to fix the barricade herself.

Gray Girl has come to nuzzle her and check the empty basket—except Clio doesn't want the mare to follow her and lead the others to the river. The day is warm, and they're likely to play in the water once they're in it.

But the mare's soft nose tickles the worst of her rage away. Clio feeds her a last bit of grass, strokes Fouli, and waves to the others, then swings her way down the path. She can hear the river before she gets to it, a rushing murmur broken only by alarm calls of birds as she approaches.

The crossing is beautiful in spring. Ruffled by an eastern breeze, the water tinkles gently over the silt ledge that stretches most of the way across the river. Dragonflies dart above, and on either side of the washed-away gully path, the banks are green with lush spring growth.

Clio and Hector have often come here to let the horses wade in cool running water, because they'll always come back rather than scramble up the steep rocks on the other side.

Thinking of Colti struggling up it in the dark wipes out all thoughts of beauty.

She'd been hoping that what she saw from the chariot yesterday was wrong and that the hole in the barricade is nothing more than goats chewing away the thorns. But the closer she gets the clearer it is.

It's much more than a hole. The carefully woven and twisted branches have been pulled out and chewed, with only the thickest ends tossed away in disgust.

Goats would always try to climb or eat the barricade. They might have eaten and pulled the thorn fence apart with their long curving horns, even though Hector said it would last until the herd was ready to move on—and he's built fences like this every year since he lived here.

But the rocks he laid across the opening have been shoved away too. Goats couldn't have rolled the rocks away.

It had to be a person.

Clio looks back over her shoulder, as if the fence breaker might be creeping up behind her. There's not a person anywhere in sight. *I knew that!* Of course she did. This was done the night before last. Whoever did it won't still be sitting around watching.

She jumps when Mika appears through the bushes across the river, another tattered picking basket on her arm. The girl's face lights up when she sees Clio, bright as if the sun god's rays have just hit it.

Clio's face lights up too. She doesn't think anyone has ever been so glad to see her.

If a person moved those rocks it had to be an adult — and almost certainly a man. There's no way this small girl could have done it.

"Goddess greet you!"

"Where are the horses?" Mika shouts back.

"On the hill with the goats."

The river's not wide, but it's loud in its rushing. Mika slides down the rocky bank and starts to wade across the pebble ridge. It's not as solid as it looks, or maybe there's a hole from Colti crossing yesterday — she stumbles and in an instant is skidding off the ridge, face down in the water.

Time slows. Six swings of Clio's crutch to the water's edge, the river lapping at her ankles, her knees, the hem of her tunic, pushing against her, trying to knock her off the ridge too. *I can't go on.*

Dropping to her knees, she grabs her crutch by the tip and holds it out as far as she can, leaning, leaning, wiggling farther forward, leaning again till her face is nearly in the water and she still can't reach Mika and the girl is still underwater.

Wiggle forward again…

Mika bursts out of the water, flailing wildly as she tries to haul herself up onto the ledge. The gravel shifts under her, sliding her back into the river. She looks dazed, as if she doesn't know how she got there, or why Clio's crawling across the silt ledge screaming for her to grab the crutch. Then she shakes her head, grabs the curved shoulder support, and lets Clio pull her back onto the ledge. She's on her knees now too. They shuffle across the rest of the way like that, each holding one end of the crutch. Mika won't let go till they've crawled right up the clay slope to the grassy bank, well out of reach of the water.

The sun is out now but the breeze is cool. Clio's tunic clings clammily to her legs and drips onto her feet. She's shivering and her skin is pimpled as a plucked duck's—but the smaller girl's body is shaking, her teeth castanet-chattering and her tongue bleeding.

"Can I see the horses?" she asks, spitting out blood.

Clio points at the scattered stones and branches. "I have to fix the barricade first."

"I'll help."

But Mika is bone thin under her wet tunic and is shaking too hard to be useful. Her tangled plaits hang like wet snakes down her back, and snot streams over her face when she coughs.

"Great Mother," Clio prays silently, "don't let her death be on my head."

"We'll go back to my house and get a sheepskin to wrap you in. You can stand by the kilns to dry."

Mika's voice is disbelieving. "You'll take me to the town?"

Were her wits washed away in the water? Clio wonders, and tries to speak encouragingly, holding her hand out again. "It's not far. We'll run, that will warm you up."

The girl looks even more confused. "You can't run!"

Clio flushes, a strange mingling of humiliation and anger. "I can hurry."

It doesn't matter. Mika's coughing too hard to move. She splutters and gasps till she's red in the face and Clio's afraid she's going to drop dead in front of her. They climb the hill very slowly, Clio holding Mika's hand tight as if she's still dragging her out of the river.

The kilns are fired, though there's no one there. Part of Clio wants Delia to see her with this little girl who treats her like the daughter of a goddess, and the other part is glad her friend won't see her coming back from the field in a sodden tunic with a dripping child. She stands Mika in the warm air between two kilns.

"Stay here to dry—I'll be right back with a sheepskin."

Mika looks panicked, clinging even tighter to Clio's hand. "I'm dry enough," she protests through clattering teeth—at least she hasn't bitten her tongue again, thinks Clio. "Let me go with you."

"There's nothing exciting to see!"

The girl stares at her in disbelief. "So much!" she whispers. "And so much noise!"

Clio had forgotten that Mika hasn't been to town since she was seven. She hears it now, the background hum that is as much part of life as the beating of her own heart: shouting, singing, talking, and laughing; a quarrel of dogs and a complaining baby; the clatter of a heavy, rock-loaded sledge dragged along the blue cobblestones; the clang of bronze from the armorers and thump of stone from the ax makers. People jostling in the street, children running, a girl with a huge bundle of dirty washing on the way to the river. The herb scent of the hills is lost here, with the stink of molten bronze overlaying the more subtle smells of cooking pots, the sea and Mika's own fishy skin. The girl stumbles as the barrage of sensations hits her.

"Come on," says Clio, and leads her to their house.

Matti is squatting on the floor of the outdoor workshop, earnestly pinching a small pot from a ball of clay. Selena is at her wheel. They are both lost in their own worlds.

"I thought you were picking stones," Clio says, surprised to see Matti home.

Matti jumps. Selena's hand slips and knocks what was going to be a tall vase—it spins off the wheel to splatter on the floor.

"Goddess bite me!" she snaps.

It's the second time Clio's ever heard her mother swear. Selena looks as shocked as Matti and Clio; their fingers flash in a united concert against evil. Mika's the only one who doesn't find it strange. Maybe she thinks this is how life is in town—flying clay and cursing mothers.

"I got lots of stones," says Matti, recovering first. "Who's that girl? Why are you wet?"

Clio steps through the open workshop door to the house. She's glad the spare sheepskins are stacked by a stool downstairs; she doesn't want Mika to see her awkwardness in climbing the ladder to the upstairs sleeping room.

"Mika fell in crossing the river to help fix the barrier," she explains.

"And you?" asks her mother.

"I pulled her out."

"Goddess be thanked you didn't both drown," says Selena.

Mika is clinging tight to Clio's free hand. She doesn't let go till Selena's wrapped her snugly in a sheepskin cloak.

"Thank you," says the girl. Looking up, she sees the house shrine and the small painted priestess with the outstretched arms.

"Is that a goddess?"

"A priestess to serve her," Clio explains. "She'll be given to the goddess at the spring festival of the full moon."

Mika's eyes grow round as a frog's.

"My grandmother made her to go to the underworld in my place—instead of a maiden."

"She made it? Out of clay—in that workshop? Is that what you do when you're not with your horses?"

Clio can't help laughing. "Apprentices only make the simplest things." She nearly adds, "And I'm not very good at it," but doesn't, overwhelmed with a wave of love and pride in her family's work. Tears rush to her eyes, sudden as the laughter. "Mama's a master of pots, everything she makes is beautiful and fine as eggshell—but this was my grandmother's last creation and no one has ever made anything like it before."

Mika reaches a hand toward the statue.

"Come out into the sunshine!" Selena snaps. The girl's hand drops.

"You won't get dry in the house," Selena adds more gently, leading her back outside. Clio wonders if she imagined it—for a moment she thought her mother wanted Mika away from the statue more than she cared about her getting dry.

Almost as if she didn't want her to see it.

That's crazy. Everyone knows about the statue. Apart from the day Clio carried it in the house goddess festival, half the town has come to see it and many have made an offering as if it was already dedicated to the Great Mother. Mika's tiny settlement might be away from the town, but it's still under the rule of the palace and the goddess.

"I need to go back to finish the fence," she says. She still can't read the reason, but Selena definitely looks relieved when Mika grabs Clio's hand, terrified of being left behind.

"You have the knife for the thorn branches?" Selena asks.

Clio panics for a moment—what if she's lost it in the river? But it's still safe in the pouch hanging from her tunic belt.

"Go with the goddess," Selena says, kissing her daughter's forehead as if she was going to sea and not on a fifteen-minute walk to the river. She says the same to Mika and kisses her too. "Go with the goddess."

The girl stiffens and steps backwards.

Does she not have any women around her, to teach her the courtesies of life? What kind of barbarians are these fishers? Clio stands very still with her hand on her heart. *Look, Mika, it's simple. Just do what I do or my mother won't even let you help me build a thorn fence.*

It's a very long moment before the younger girl follows.

Selena sighs. Her face is as expressionless as the Lady's white-painted mask. Only her eyes betray her—though Clio's not sure whether she's reading anger or fear.

Luckily, Mika doesn't speak again until they are back on the river road. "If it wasn't for the statue, would the Lady really sacrifice a girl?"

"Yes."

"Why?"

"Because that's what the oracle says the goddess wants."

"What will the goddess do with a dead girl?"

A question with no answer. A question so huge Clio shakes it from her mind and decides she didn't hear.

> Her heart swells with pity
>   for this child of no learning,
>   a girl not so many years
>   from becoming a woman

but younger in wisdom than Matti.
It swells with rage
    that Selena did not hide her mistrust
    of a girl who'd risked herself
    to aid the horses
    and Clio.
But most of all,
    her heart swells with fear
    because a girl like this—
    a barbarian who doesn't know
    how to honor the goddess,
    does not pray with hand on heart
    or thank the god-spirit of human kindness;
    does not, perhaps,
    offer a gift of food and drink
    each time she eats—
    a girl like this
    can raise the gods to fury.
The gods, as Leira always said,
    are not fair.
    They don't care if all the land
    performs the rites
    if one person tramples
    respect in the mud.

Now it's not just Clio's heart swelling but her head spinning. What if she's the only person who knows about this family of barbarians who don't honor the goddess?

If the Lady knew, she would ask the oracle what to

do—and Clio can guess what the oracle would answer, in its riddling god words. Sacrifice.

Maybe it would decide Mika was old enough to be the spring sacrifice herself, or maybe two girls would be offered; whatever it said, she thinks Mika would die.

But Grandmother Leira created the statue so that no girl would die. She wouldn't have cared that Mika was a fisher girl from outside the town.

Leira used to say that even a slave's life is a life to be lived, though it's true that if the Lady or the chief died before their time, it would cause more change to the town than the death of fifty slaves.

"Which doesn't mean," she'd added, "that the gods value one soul over the other. Maybe they think the true value of a life is that it's given to the full. All I know is that I've lived as priest-folk, slave, and master crafter, and though my life was different, my soul was the same for each."

She said it very quietly, even in their own home with the door closed for the night. She said they must never repeat it, only live it.

It was lived when strangers came by the workshop to pay her reverence as if she were a priestess, because they came from the island that died, and Leira was the only person who still held that land's sacred stories and songs. When she fled here, she thought she and her mother and grandmother were the only ones left alive, but over the years more searched her out: traders or crafters who'd been abroad when the war of the gods began, and others who'd sailed just in time. The Lady of those days decreed that Leira must never say where she'd come from, for fear that the townfolk would realize that their priest-folk could tumble too. But of course people still knew the story, and Selena says that's why the Lady listened to her after the oracle.

CHAPTER 7
THE VOICE FROM THE
UNDERWORLD

If Clio can't
    rescue slaves from the stink of purple
    or create a statue to serve a goddess
    and save a girl's life,
    maybe she still can
    please the Great Mother
    and save the town.
The thought huge in her head,
    bursting to escape—
    her fingers flash against evil
    to keep it hidden.
Because who is she—
    not yet a woman,
    an apprentice never likely to be
    master of her craft—
    who is she to save the town?
But through her thoughts

comes a voice so loud she jumps and stumbles;
    drops her crutch:
    You will do what you must!
The voice of a girl her age,
    faint accent of an island home;
    a voice she knows as old and frail
    though her heart recognizes
    what cannot be true—
    Clio hears her grandmother, young again.
Strangest of all
    is the calm that descends
    so she cannot be afraid
    of the voice of the dead.
So she instructs the barbarian girl
    that before they start their work
    they'll thank the goddess of trees
    for the branches they cut.
"Is there a god for horses?" Mika asks
    and Clio tries to explain
    the web of gods who rule the earth
    with the Great Mother of all.
Tongue loosened now,
    Mika chatters as they work:
    it was her brother who told her
    a horse had crossed the river.
    She doesn't say why
    or how he knew.
Her brother is older
    by a good five summers;
    they live alone—

their father and mother dead
and the houses of their aunts
too crowded for more.
Without a boat,
Mika fishes from the shore,
collects shell creatures from rocks
while her brother dives deep
to where octopus hide.
And though they used to
trade fish to the town
they sell mostly now
to settlers up west—
she doesn't know who these settlers are.
A life without friends and folk all round—
a story as strange to Clio
as a false note in a song
or thumb-dent in a pot.
But she knows nothing of fishers' lives
or small settlements along the coast
so the thought glides away
like a snake into grass,
lost in the rush
of wrapping capes around arms,
protection from the branches of thorns
she cuts with her small bronze knife.
Levering a rock into place
at each side of the gully—
they leave the rest, too heavy to move—
drive in branches across the mouth
and weave thorn saplings between.

Even with the sheepskin guards
    blood spatters their tunics
    till it looks like they've offered
    more than song to the gods.
Clio hopes the blood pleases them—
    Great Mother, tree goddess
    and god of horses and sea—
    so they'll keep her horses
    safe and contained.
The sun halfway to setting before they're done,
    but Mika asks to see the horses—
    they're still with the goats
    and Petros is back,
    staring strangely as they approach.
"The fence is done," says Clio,
    "and the horses should stay."
Petros stares at blood-spattered tunics
    and bleeding hands
    as if he can't believe that anyone
    would build a thorn fence for no reason
    except to see a horse again
    and stroke its neck.
The girl doesn't ask
    to feed Gray Girl or Fouli
    but the filly and colt eat from her hand,
    Colti nibbling at her hair—
    Clio didn't know his love
    was so easily won.
    With a jolt she guesses
    yesterday was not the first time

the girl has fed him—
and when Mika strokes his face
from small white star to whiskered nose
down neck and back, leaning close—
her yearning to slide on
so plain to see it's clear she's spied
Hector on the horse's back.
Rage building in Clio
hot and glowing
because this is her father's horse
and no thieving girl should ride him first—
if anyone does, it should be her.
Anger making her forget
she'll never ride again,
Hector may never come back
and she may not be here
to greet him if he does.
Burying her face in Gray Girl's soft neck
she is shaken by tears
for what will happen to the horses
if she goes underground
before her father returns.
Breathing in deep
till the sweet smell of horse sweat
says what she must do.
Mika's been spying—
but no thief would bother
to herd strayed horses home
or build a fence to keep them in—
as Petros said,

building a thorn fence is not much fun.
Clio must bind her to the herd
to keep them safe.
And though it tears at her heart
she knows the way to bind this girl
surer than chains.
"If you come back," says Clio,
wiping her eyes on her tunic sleeve,
"I'll teach you to ride."

Petros has more to say after Mika's gone. He shows Clio his hands, grazed raw from moving rocks for the wall.

"My sister's first child is coming," he adds. As Clio guessed, their mother is with her, singing life into being as it emerges from the dark womb. The midwife will be there too, but who can sing with more heart than the mother of the laboring woman, grandmother of the child to come?

They go back to the problem of guarding the animals with the palace's new demands. "We can't leave them on their own—we'll lose them all!"

They both remember what the Lady said to Cross-eye the shepherd.

"It doesn't matter to the palace who owns the animals," Petros says dully, "they'll still get their share. There are no excuses for lookout duty anymore, either. We can build the wall one day and be on lookout the next."

"But now you've met Mika…she could be trained, surely, if her clan would let her go."

"I still say you can't trust those fishers."

"She's a child, no more than ten summers. And brave—I told you how she jumped in front of the colt to turn him."

"I didn't say they weren't brave. I said you can't trust them. My brother says…"

"*My brother says,*" Clio mimics cruelly. "You'd think your brother was a priest, the way you quote him."

"So tell me why they didn't report the ship you saw?" Petros snaps. "It must have gone right past them."

"They probably thought the town would see it—and then they might have heard it had been reported, so they didn't need to." It doesn't sound convincing, even to her.

"All I'm saying is, don't trust her just because she likes horses."

"And I'm saying you didn't see her running to head Colti off when she could have sent him the other way!" *Or the admiration in her eyes when she looks at me.* Petros doesn't need to know the last one.

Evening comes,
    the rising moon a reminder
    this long day is almost gone—
    one less remaining
    till sacrifice and spring.
But in this moment
    there is Matti leaning on her knee,
    a supper of the greens she's picked,

fish Mama traded for
and their cup of ale—
singing praise to Great Mother
till the hymn flows
over the priestess in the shrine
standing with the small and humble
goddess of the home—
surely with both of them there
no harm can come.
Though in the bright light of morning,
shaping feast cups between wet palms,
Clio wonders again
if they'll be for the feast
of her own death.
The thought knocking the tray
of cups from her hands—
scooping up the ruins,
she grabs her crutch and flees
before her mother can speak.
Hurries not to her horses
but her grandmother's grave
with an offering of lilies, tiny and yellow,
picked along the way.
She wants Leira to promise
the oracle will accept the statue;
the goddess will honor it,
with peace and plenty;
Dada will return safe
and she'll be here to greet him.
No answer comes; not a sound or a sign.

Leira always loved flowers
but maybe they're not what she wants—
not from Clio
not right now.
"Thank you for your gift,"
Clio says as she has before,
tears clouding her eyes
remembering her grandmother pour
her life into the clay—
and now Clio sees
what she must offer in return.
"If I live," she says,
past the spring full moon,
grow to be a woman when autumn comes,
I must make my choice
and work to be master of my craft.
"My horses will never be of real use—
what could I carry
in a chariot so light
I can tow it myself?
No matter how I love them
I see they are Dada's fate
and not mine.
"So my offering to you,"
she tells her dear, dead grandmother,
"is to work at my craft—
the craft that was yours,
bringing the skill of my hands
and the love of my heart
to all I create,

as the only way
I can honor you."
But Leira stays silent,
as if this is still
not what she wants.
And when Clio returns
to replace the smashed cups
throwing clay on her wheel
with all the care she can give,
Selena smiles an empty smile
and sends her away:
"Go, child; I can do all that's needed.
Were you not intending
to check your horses today?"
As if her daughter's best
is still not good enough
and she doesn't want her there.

Selena decides they should join in the town life as usual, instead of staying home and worrying, so from now on they'll go to the dawn ceremony in turns—but first they greet the house goddess and the clay priestess. Selena lights an oil lamp between the two little statues and they hold hands and sing, too quietly for neighbors to hear, but loud enough for the goddess.

The work of the feast cups goes on. Used for one night only, smashed at the end of the feast, so there's no need to fire them. Head and Tail the carrier twins take the trays of dried cups to the palace; the ones from the day before are still on their racks, but the rest have gone. It's a relief when each tray leaves and they don't have to worry that Clio's crutch or Matti's jumping will knock and smash them.

To keep her promise to Leira, Clio wants to start learning something new, a tall urn or a spouted jug—she's never made a jug with a good spout—but Selena is slow to teach her, sending her off to the horses each morning. There's been nothing to take to the kilns since the ships left, and the days that it's Clio's turn to go to the palace for the dawn ceremony, Delia has been at the opposite side of the court with her own mother and they haven't been able to speak. Clio wishes she knew if it was because Delia didn't want to.

Except it's better not to know because she couldn't bear it if her friend doesn't want to talk to her.

It's not just Delia; it's Delia's mama too—and all the mothers with girls their age, the fourteen of them who are nearly-women. They keep their daughters tight beside them, buzzing like angry bees at the world around.

All except Selena, who is as happy for Clio to be with her horses as Hector could be.

CHAPTER 8
MIKA AND COLTI

The moon was a slim silver crescent when the ships sailed. Now there's only a sliver of darkness to be eaten before its face grows full again, just three more nights. And that will be the beginning of the last cycle before the spring festival. Clio shivers, counting it down.

The feast cups are nearly finished. Soon Clio and Selena, along with Aunt Fotia's studio and Delia and her mother, will have to take their turns at wall building or whatever else the palace needs. The creation of beautiful pots to be traded next year or after they have survived the raiders—if they survive the raiders, if there's a next year—doesn't seem very important anymore. All Clio can focus on is training Mika, pouring her knowledge into the younger girl so that some part of her own spirit will live on if she doesn't.

"Go," her mother says whenever she can, because even if Selena doesn't understand Hector and Clio's passion for the horses, she does understand it's a passion. Angry, anxious, and overwhelmed as she is, what she cares about more than anything is keeping her daughter safe. Keeping her happy is a very close second. She just wishes that she could show it better, because so often when she says, "Go!" she knows that Clio hears, "Go! Get out of my sight!"

The truth is that she'd keep Clio sitting tight beside her every minute of the day if her daughter could be content doing that. But the closer the time comes, the less she believes that the oracle will accept the statue in the place of a living girl. Even if it does, the goddess may not win against the raiders and their war gods. The horses may be stolen and she and her daughter killed or sold into slavery. If these are the last days of her daughter's life, Selena wants them to be happy.

So Clio goes, and somehow Mika eludes her brother, and they meet by the herder's hut soon after dawn every morning. Petros watches, bemused by their dedication to these beautiful but useless animals at this perilous time. And though he can't help being impressed by the fisher girl's genuine care for the horses, it doesn't ease his suspicion about her motives.

But this morning, when the girls have just arrived and Petros is leaving for the wall, he describes where the goats are grazing and where he wants them to stay. The old dog is with him. "He won't work for anyone else," says Petros. None of them mention that the old dog doesn't really work even for him anymore.

"You want me to watch them?" asks Mika, her eyes bright in disbelief.

"Clio can tell you what to do," says Petros, handing Mika his flute on its leather cord. "This might help."

Clio is nearly as touched as Mika. She'd been given a flute while she still wasn't able to move after her accident. It had been something to look at, to hold and feel, and best of all, something new she could learn. For the time that she was playing, it took away the pain and fear. It's one of her most prized possessions, but she's never brought it to the field because the horses had already learned her cuckoo whistle and she didn't want to confuse the goats.

And until she looked at the one Petros has just handed Mika, she never realized that he had made hers. "I'll bring mine," she says. "We'll do our best."

She starts Mika's training with the most basic horse care, showing her how to run her hands over Colti's and Fleet Foot's spines and down their legs to feel for prickles or cuts, how to use the fine wooden feather comb on their backs and the wide toothed one on their manes; how to scrape off lather with a wooden blade or rub a light sweat off with dry grass. She shows her how to check their hooves, and how to flick out pebbles or thorns with a small pointed pick.

Fleet Foot is still wary, but Clio's shocked to see that Colti allows Mika to handle his feet. Shocked but happy, because it's difficult for her to balance with the weight of a horse's hoof in her hand, and although she's checked them every day since her father left, she's been very relieved that none of the horses have had a problem for her to deal with yet.

You are on your path, says a voice in her head. The voice that sounds like a younger version of Leira, that she can't argue with.

She'd never realized she knew so much until she had to teach someone else. Suddenly this knowledge is molten gold trapped in her head, needing to find its way out to be shared.

"If you're going to ride Colti, you need to learn to put his bridle on."

Or should she teach Mika on gentle Gray Girl first?

No. The answer is clear: there's no time. Mika must learn on Colti or not at all. Clio holds out the bridle and shows Mika the smooth bronze jointed bit.

"This goes in his mouth. Make sure the reins are straight and at the back. Put one hand here, between his ears so he doesn't throw his head up; hold the bit to his mouth…slide it in when he starts mouthing—and then this strap over the ears."

Mika's head is exactly the same height as Colti's withers. He allows the girl to hold his head and slip the bridle on.

"Hold the reins in one hand, at the shoulder, so you don't yank his head as you get on. Stand on this rock so you're higher…"

Mika's already gone around to Colti's left side. Holding the reins as Clio told her, she puts her right hand a little farther down his back, jumps to pull herself up and swing her right leg over. It's a little clumsy, but she's done it—and Colti hasn't moved.

"You've got up on him before!"

"Sort of," Mika mutters, wriggling into place on the smooth dark back. "He was standing beside a rock...I just slid on. But I fell off when he started moving. It was the day before I met you."

"The day before the wild dogs."

She would have taken Colti if I hadn't searched for him. If Gray Girl had crossed, she'd have taken her. Clio feels sick and awed at the same time. Losing Gray Girl would feel like the end of her life.

Mika twists her fingers into the colt's wiry mane. "I don't know anything about the wild dogs except what you told me." She doesn't mention her suspicions, or that one of the settlement's dogs is missing—or that her brother had hit her hard enough to knock her down when she'd asked about it. But not mentioning any of it also means she can't tell Clio that she's refused to answer her brother's questions about the horses or where she disappears to every morning. She never leaves till he's started diving, but she still feels that he's watching her.

She doesn't care. He's not going to stop her coming to the horses—nothing's going to stop her. Especially now that she's sitting on this beautiful colt. Actually riding.

Clio knows she's hiding something, but decides to go on trusting Leira's voice—which means trusting Mika.

She returns to the lesson. "Turn your leg like this," she says, moving the girl's leg so that her foot is pointing forward and her thigh sitting more smoothly along the colt's body. "You can hold onto his mane for now, but riding means holding on with your legs. Touch him with your calves to move forward—you'll never need to kick him. And talk to him. He'll listen."

Clio hasn't led a bridled horse since her accident; even before she'd have only led Gray Girl a few paces to the mounting rock. It's awkward because her own gait is uneven, with a slight hesitation between her left arm throwing the crutch forward and the right leg following. The colt jerks his head every time.

It's not just Mika and Colti learning together: Clio has to learn how to teach them. She lengthens the rein. That's better—the colt is happier; she doesn't feel as tense.

Mika breathes out, something between a hiccup and a squeak. Clio glances back—she's been concentrating so hard on keeping the colt moving smoothly that the girl could have fallen off without her noticing.

But Mika's still firmly on the horse's back, her mouth a round O, eyes shining and her whole dirty face alive with joy.

It's worth it, thinks Clio. *This is the right thing to do.* This time the voice is her own.

When Clio's with the horses, concentrating on figuring out all that she knows and how to share it with someone, there's no time to think of anything else.

But as she turns homeward on the river road, the sight of the town's west wall throws her back into the fearful present. The wall is growing, but it's not as tall as the three other sides. How high does a wall have to be to keep out an enemy? Higher than this, Clio guesses. It's not much above her head—she could scramble over it herself if she had two good legs.

She's not surprised to hear there was a new announcement after she left this morning. Work on the wall will be picked up even more—everyone except the metal forgers will give every second day of their labor. The only thing that matters is to have as many people as possible building all the time. The purple slaves will labor at night, every night, lit by torches. They will return to the purple works to sleep when the Lady calls the dawn.

Anyone not fit to work on the wall can collect spring greens and shellfish for the workers to eat. Babies will be cared for in groups, one mother or grandmother looking after several infants so the mothers can work. Petros's mother and another grandmother, who are keeping the thirty-day vigil with their daughters and newborns, will have other babies brought to their homes each morning.

The town rings with renewed urgency. The hammering of the stone ax makers seems more booming; the hissing of molten bronze being poured into moulds more sinister; even the soft rasp of whet stones sharpening knives and scythes—every sword in the palace has already been sharpened to its finest edge—sounds more harsh and grating than it ever has before. Children cry more and laugh less; dogs are as quarrelsome as their owners, growling and barking for no reason.

"Aunt Fotia will share the vigil with us again," says Selena. "She and I will go to the wall on different days so you can still care for your horses."

But Clio goes first, this very day —
    Selena is old,
    Fotia older,
    her grandson born the same year as Clio —
    old bones will suffer
    pushing, rolling rocks from the earth.
    Clio, despite her dragging leg,
    is young and strong —
    an almost-woman —
    and will take her place
    no matter what her grandmother says
    in her oracle voice from the land of death.
And, piping shrill beside Leira's words
    are Delia's, from dawn a day before:
    "What hardship," she snarled,
    "to gather greens in the hills
    while you visit your horses
    with your new little friend."
Sharp as a face slap,
    the words knocked Clio's arm
    back from her friend's
    because they're true —
    there's no chore she prefers

to gathering wild greens;
true as well
that the horses she loves
are no chore at all—
but she couldn't explain
that Mika's training is a different bond,
a different part of Clio herself
than the one she's shared
with the friend of her heart
her whole life through.
A barest mumbled good-bye;
as she turned from Delia,
hurrying to her grandmother's grave
with no offering but
a single spring crocus found on the way
and no question clear in her mind
though many were tearing
at her heart.
Grass already furred over Leira's grave
and as she sat by it,
gathering breath and thoughts,
a cloud darkened the sky—
a chattering, wheeling, ragged cloud
of swallows returning for spring—
and it seemed they hovered
around where she sat
so through their squeaking
she heard her grandmother's voice,
"Your way is new,
something not easy

to explain or to do—
    but it has its own import
    and it is yours."
Hesitant now,
    joining men and women from their quarter
    trooping to the rocky slope
    between cemetery and town,
    gladness leaping in her heart
    at a tap on her shoulder:
    Delia beside her
    as if they've never been apart.
The women are squatting,
    working hard and fast, puffing and cursing,
    to pry rocks from the ground
    and roll them to sledges
    pulled by strong men or palace oxen.
Clio finds a rock—
    as long her arm from shoulder to wrist—
    left-leg-kneels at its face
    right leg stretching awkward behind,
    and with her smooth stone trowel
    begins to scrape and dig around it—
    like a dog after a buried bone,
    flicking dirt over face and tunic,
    and Delia digging at the other side—
    not so fast or furious as Clio,
    not knowing it's a race.
With a long strong stick
    they poke under the rock
    one side then another

till with a grunt Clio pries it loose —
it's bigger now than it looked before —
and it tumbles over,
once, twice, down the hill.
Standing to shout for a sledge,
Delia slips and stumbles,
landing on outstretched hands —
and her grazed palms bleed.
Clio pulls her up
and shoulder to shoulder on the hill
they watch Cousin Miso and his friend
shove their rock to a sledge
to be hauled to the wall
while they hug their truce and cry.

Although she still doesn't know exactly what Leira's words mean, Clio is smiling as she turns onto the goat path next morning.

Then she sees Colti and Fleet Foot. Petros must be on the wall again — the two young horses are chasing the flock around the field, up the hill toward the peak, scattering them wildly.

Clio whistles her cuckoo call. By now the horses have raced even higher up than the goats, too far away for her whistle to reach them — or they are having too much fun to listen — but when it's echoed from the herder's hut, the colt hears. He stops for a moment, proud on the hill, his head high and searching for where the sound came from. When he hears it again he neighs and the filly stops too.

Clio rushes up the path, pausing only to whistle. Mika echoes her from the hut and the two horses start to trot down the hill. As they reach the scattered flock, they gallop around them—and miraculously push them back toward the corner where Petros wanted them.

Gray Girl neighs bossily before eating the grasses Clio offers her. The colt and filly trot up as if they'd meant to meet them all along. The girls look at each other and burst out laughing.

"Petros told me he'd seen Colti tease the goats," says Clio, "but I thought he was exaggerating. Now Fleet Foot's doing it too!"

"He's so beautiful," says Mika, who can't hear any criticism of the horse she adores. "And isn't it the spirit of the horse god that makes him play like that?"

"Maybe," says Clio, "but we need the god spirit to leave him now so you can ride."

She decides that a lunging rein is the best way to back up the prayer. Hector had used it in the winter to let Colti feel some control before he had the weight of a man on his back.

Bridling the colt and knotting the reins over his neck, she attaches the lunging rope to his bit and clucks for him to move, feeding out the rein and pivoting with her crutch as he breaks into his smooth, rocking trot.

He's clearly calmer after two rounds; after the third Clio leads him to the mounting rock.

She holds him still while Mika pulls herself on. Her mounting is already smoother than the day before.

"Don't worry about the reins," Clio tells her. "Today you're just learning to stay on."

"Like yesterday," Mika points out.

"Yes. But I was leading him yesterday and we just walked. Now you're going to trot." She checks that Mika's legs are in the right position, reminds her to grip, and tells Colti to move on.

Mika is concentrating so hard she's almost grimacing, though a smile keeps breaking through. Then, just as she's settled into the movement of the trot, Colti begins to canter—and she lands on the ground.

She picks herself up quickly, and it's not till Clio has brought the horse to a full stop that she realizes Mika is crying.

"Are you hurt?"

Mika shakes her head. "I'm sorry," she sobs. "I didn't mean to!"

"I know you didn't mean to! Believe me, I've never meant to fall off but I've done it more times than I can count!"

"You're not angry?"

"Angry because you fell? Why would I be?"

"Because you're trying so hard to teach me and I've failed," the younger girl wails.

Clio stares at her. She suspects that the differences between their lives are more than the difference between their villages. It's not just that Hector would never have been angry at her for falling off Gray Girl—Selena has never punished her even when her carelessness has ruined a pot.

"In my father's land they say, 'A rider who has never fallen is a better liar than rider.'"

Mika stares at her for a long moment, and slowly breaks into a smile. "Can I try again?"

"That's the only way you'll learn to ride."

CHAPTER 9
TWENTY-FOUR NIGHTS
TILL THE FULL MOON

The sling stones collected by the youngest children are heaped near the gates, at points along the wall, and even at the palace entrance—though if the raiders get in as far as the palace, there'll be no room to whirl a rope.

Matti collects them for home as well. He brings back so many Clio and Selena suspect he's stolen them from the nearest pile. The heap at the end of his bed is too high to step over.

"Clio and I don't know how to use a sling," Selena reminds him.

"I'm going to learn," Matti insists. "Petros is going to teach me."

"When did you talk to Petros about that?"

"Last time he came to the waking-up-the-sun."

Clio thinks it might be a very good idea for Matti to start learning now--she wishes she'd gone on practicing when Petros tried to teach her.

But Selena scoops the little boy up in her arms, hugging him till he struggles and squirms. "Goddess willing, let us have peace before this one is old enough to be a warrior!"

"You can fill a pouch to give Petros to protect the goats," Clio tells him.

"And the horses!" Matti protests.

"And the horses," agrees Mama, and distracts him by asking him to roll out long snakes of clay to start a pot.

In the day
    it's easy to believe
    that all will be well
    because Selena says it will
    and the men are practicing javelins,
    spears, and archery
    and more weapons are made
    every day.
But most of all because
    Grandmother Leira worked so hard
    to create this priestess of clay—
    and all the goddess has to do
    is speak through the oracle
    to accept the gift
    and Clio, with all the girls of town,
    can stay alive and breathing
    above the earth.
But in demon dreams she feels the clay
    not rolling between her palms

but sliding into her mouth
and throat,
choking, suffocating—
and she cannot shout
because she is nothing but clay,
a silent scream within the earth.
Sometimes
Selena hears her struggles,
holds her, wakes her,
wipes the sweat from her forehead,
and soothes her like a child.
Yet demon dreams scorn soothing,
mock a mother's touch—
return with sharp-edged swords,
a sacrificial ax,
and blood dripping from an altar stone.
Or tell a tale
of what will happen
if the goddess is not honored—
dreaming that Clio had sailed
with her father on the ship
while at home
all that he feared came true—
raiders pouring through the town,
long swords slashing,
sharp daggers stabbing,
heavy clubs pounding,
the warriors' own heads protected
by tusk-covered caps;
shields over their bodies

as they throw flares into houses,
smash the Great Mother's home
and drag women and children
to be sold as slaves.
  She sees her father swimming,
diving from the ship,
struggling back to save them
until he drowns.
  Some nights the demons
leave her to sleep
and invade her mama instead.
  Clio wakes to her cries,
holds her mother as Selena holds her
huddling on one mat
singing into the dark
until their hearts beat calm
and their eyes can close.

"Take Matti with you this morning," says Selena. They are singing the dawn quietly at home so Clio can leave before the work parties start.

Clio sees that Selena is utterly exhausted. When she's kissed them good-bye she climbs the ladder back up to the sleeping room. Clio's never seen her mother in bed after dawn.

Matti is skipping as they near the herder's hut. Petros is a heroic figure to the little boy, living out on the hills with the animals—and best of all, defending them with his sling.

"I brought you this pouch of stones," he says, "but you've got rocks everywhere!"

"We do," agrees Petros. "But it's not easy to find the best ones." He picks up a jagged chunk of granite, fits it into the sling's leather pouch, and whirrs the rope over his head. The stone falls short and wide of his target.

Matti doesn't know what to say. His hero has failed.

Reaching into the pouch on his belt, Petros pulls out a river stone, round and smooth as an egg. This time he hits the target tree hard, again and again until all twelve stones are at the foot of the tree.

"Stones like eggs—those are what we need."

"I could make you some."

"You can make rocks, my little friend?"

"That's silly!" exclaims Matti. "Only gods can make rocks. But I can make clay eggs."

"I think that's a very good idea," says Petros.

Mika arrives. Matti is shy of her and stays with Petros, who is showing him how to whirl the rope without any projectiles in it. "We practice first," he explains, "so we don't kill anyone by mistake."

Matti looks so alarmed that Petros changes it. "I mean *hurt*. We don't want to hurt anyone."

Clio and Mika decide that Petros doesn't need to know about Colti and Fleet Foot chasing the goats yesterday. They groom the horses and Mika rides Colti on the lunge line again—without falling off.

"Tomorrow you can ride him on your own," says

Clio. "But you must have other chores—doesn't your brother mind you coming every day? Aren't you supposed to be fishing?"

"He doesn't seem to care," says Mika. "I'm sure he knows I'm going somewhere—but he just tells me to get out of the house in the morning and keep away from where he's fishing. Dymos has a quick temper and a strong arm, and I do what he says."

Over the past days, she's let slip more details of her life in the tiny settlement, and of her brother. The girl he was to marry died in the sickness last winter, as did the aunt they lived with. Their father survived it then died suddenly two moons later. Clio is overwhelmed by the girl's loneliness.

But Colti is filling that gap. His dark coat gleams with the rubbing she gives him each day, and she picks him so many greens that he whickers and runs to her as soon as she appears. It's hard to believe that she hasn't known him for a half moon cycle. And though the dark worm of jealousy hasn't completely disappeared, Clio's mostly glad to see their bond.

Besides, not even beautiful Colti can compare to her own dear Gray Girl. As she harnesses the mare after Mika's lesson, Clio feels a surge of love for the horse she has grown up with, for her steadiness and willingness to try something new.

Matti runs up. "You said I could go with you when you know how to drive."

"I'm learning," says Clio, "but I'm not ready for a passenger yet."

Matti runs back to his sling practice and Clio steps into her chariot.

The driving is a bit easier, a bit smoother; even with so many people watching both she and the mare are more relaxed.

It's not till they're on their way home that Clio wonders why Mika's brother doesn't care that his sister disappears every morning and isn't bringing home as many shellfish as she should.

CHAPTER 10
THE BALANCE OF LIGHT
AND DARK

It's the morning of the equinox. Some years the full
moon comes the next night. "Thank the goddess,"
says Selena, "that the moon is still so early in its cycle
this year. Twenty-one days till its fullness brings the
festival."

She wipes away angry tears, which Clio pretends
not to see. Clio doesn't want to count down the days.
Better to concentrate on the horses and their training.

Petros and the goats are on the second hill. Mika
isn't here yet, but Gray Girl, Fouli, and Fleet Foot are
down near the river. They turn at her whistle and trot
toward her. The colt isn't with them.

Has he crossed again? What if I've lost him?

*No, he's there, coming back on the track from the
river road—where's he been? He's afraid of the bridge,
he'd never go there alone.*

There's something on his back.

It's Mika.

The girl sees her at the same moment, and even from here Clio can tell that she's wondering whether to jump off and pretend she was never there. In the end she stays on. She even stays on when the colt sees Gray Girl nuzzling Clio for greens and breaks into a trot to get his share. Clio picks some quickly, hardly aware of what she's doing. *Mika is truly riding!*

Riding Colti, who Hector was going to start training in the autumn. Riding after these few days of practice, without the years of getting to know the horse, without a bridle or reins. Without Clio's permission or help.

Isn't that what training's for? asks a small voice at the back of her mind.

Not yet! Clio snaps back.

Jealousy spears through her, black and spreading as octopus ink. She wants to shout at Mika to get off, but as her mouth opens, that other voice comes into her head. *A swallow with a cuckoo chick in its nest will rejoice in teaching it to fly.*

Her grandmother didn't speak in riddles when she was alive. Clio wishes she hadn't started just because she's dead.

"What are you doing?" she demands. A stupid question but all she can think of.

"I asked the colt," says Mika. "He said yes."

Clio's anger trickles away—and though there's still a black smear of jealousy, her body is filling and prickling with the golden glow of awe. Mika can communicate with the horses. The colt is happy under her, just as calm as with Hector. Maybe even calmer.

It hurts to admit but there's something exciting about it too...it's Clio who's teaching her. Mika's gift with the horses would never be fulfilled without her.

Yes! says the Leira voice.

So that's as important as she feels it is. She'll understand later, when it's time.

She stands in front of the colt with her hand on her heart. "Thank you for carrying Mika."

The girl looks surprised, but Clio's not finished.

"Thank you, Great Mother, for showing Mika how to talk to Colti. Thank you for the work that Mika and Colti will do together, whatever the cost."

"What do you mean?" Mika asks in alarm.

"I don't know." Clio drops her suddenly heavy praying hand; she can hardly remember what she's just said, as if she's just woken from a dream.

Petros is on lookout duty again. His mother is still at home with her daughter and twelve-day-old grandson, so the goats are unattended and wandering. Three does and their newly born kids are locked in the enclosure; some are grazing nearby—but several have disappeared. Clio didn't see them as she came down the river road.

"They haven't been near the hut since I've been here," says Mika, brushing Colti's dark flanks. She's already checked his hooves for stones.

"I'll drive down to the river and the track to the bridge." Clio says it calmly, ignoring the whirling butterflies in her belly. She can do this, she knows she can. She'll have to be careful—chasing the goats with the chariot might frighten them into a stampede—but she could go around and block them from crossing the bridge while Mika herds from behind.

She's imagining Mika on foot—but when she finishes hooking up the chariot, Mika's bridled Colti and is on his back.

"Herding goats is a lot harder than just riding down the path," Clio warns. "They'll race everywhere and the horse will turn sharp to head them off. So rein him in if he's going too fast; hang onto his mane if you think you're going to fall—but it's your legs that will keep you on."

Mika nods, her eyes shining. Her thin legs stick out from her grimy tunic, where she's tucked it under her bottom. Her toes are pointing forward, not bouncing outward the way they were the first times she got on him. Suddenly, stronger than the jealousy, pride glows through Clio: a pride for this strange little fisher girl and Hector's horse.

She drives Gray Girl down the goat track to the river; Colti and Mika go across the field, and Fouli and Fleet Foot gallop excitedly between.

Driving is still much harder than riding. She has to concentrate every moment—on holding the reins, just tight enough that she can feel the mare's mouth but not too tight; on keeping her balance in the seat, and watching the track ahead as well as the twitch of Gray Girl's ears...she can barely look farther to scan the field for the missing goats.

There's one! And another! High up on the peak; they're scattered all over it, as if hoping the tumbles of rock might have miraculously sprouted grass. Clio can't decide if goats are crazy because they try to eat anything and anywhere, or if they're clever because somehow they always find food in the craziest places and survive. But smart or crazy, they're not supposed to be here: she needs to get them down the hill and along the river to their own field.

The rocks are too big for the chariot to go over; too close together for it to go between.

"I see them!" Mika calls.

And before Clio can decide what to do, Mika's turned Colti and is trotting up the hill. She goes wide, as if she's been herding goats all her life—and Colti does the rest. He weaves his way through the stones to come down on the flock from above. All Mika needs to do is stay on.

"Come on, Gray Girl!" Clio lifts the reins and they follow the path up the river. She studies the fork in the trail ahead. If the goats are feeling contrary as they run down, they could take the arm into thick shrub instead of following the river home. She heads Gray Girl up the hill trail until the undergrowth is too dense to go on, and turns. By the time they're facing back down the path the goats are nearly at the fork.

Gray Girl stamps and twitches. She doesn't know

what they're doing and doesn't like standing still while goats are pouring down the hill.

But when the first ones turn and stream toward them, Clio clucks for the mare to move forward. "Gently," she tells her. "We want them to turn, not panic."

She concentrates on keeping her hands firm on the reins. Gray Girl wants to rush at them—as long as they're running from her, she doesn't care how they scatter. But Clio needs them to turn onto the path to the river.

The first ones do.

Then three yearling bucks start up the track toward her, pawing and ready to charge. Gray Girl stamps too and the goats spin around to race straight back up the hill they've come from.

"Ha!" shouts Mika, sliding from side to side as Colti picks his way down the hill toward the bucks. But somehow she stays on, and the bucks turn and trot after the rest of their flock.

Mika is grinning. So is Clio.

"Go wide!" she calls. "I'll take the path."

The goats are on their way home now; they barely need herding. But Mika and Colti trot beside them and Clio drives from behind—not long before noon, all the goats are back in their field.

Petros returns while they're rubbing the horses down. Clio's so shaky she has to lean on Gray Girl as well as her crutch—she didn't know you could shake with relief, and she also didn't know she'd been so afraid: for her chariot, her horse, herself, and for Mika. Or maybe just afraid of failing, of being useless. All she knows for sure is that she is warm with joy—and Mika obviously feels the same. Her legs are shaky too, and she's waddling with pain after the long rough ride— but her sweaty face is aglow with joy.

"I saw you!" Petros exclaims. "You herded the goats back! Where were they?"

Clio tells him. Mika is suddenly tongue tied again.

"The chariot isn't right for herding—but we did it together!"

Petros turns to Mika with his hand on his heart. "Thank you."

Driving
    everything else disappears;
    her mind has no room
    but for honest, fleeting fears—
    guts clenching with rocking wheels—
    and all the feeling, seeing, hearing, doing
    that driving demands,
    empty the worries
    and fill her with life.
But, starting as she leaves the field,
    swinging her way up the river road,
    darker fears return
    swirling clouds of worry,
    till by the north gates
    the cicada hum of townfolk
    shrills through her bones like an off-key flute.

Passing down the street,
    on every side,
    from every workshop floor,
    every open-windowed house,
    float whispered rumors of fear and dread.
"The chief won't share what the messengers say."
    "Omens of grief
    in our sister town across the bay—
    though the raiders are nearer us than them."
The mothers at the well
    care only for the sacrifice;
    those whose daughters are past Clio's age
    saying, "One life for so many,
    if the goddess decrees it—
    if it were me, I'd rejoice
    to save the town."
Others hold their babies tight,
    carry toddlers old enough to walk,
    and the mothers of her friends
    are not rejoicing
    at all
    but are sick with fear—
    as if they've forgotten the offered statue
    or that sacrifice is always
    from Leira's line.
Then words that fill her heart with ice,
    Delia's mother:
    "The Ladies always had some fear of Leira,
    born to priest-folk, then a slave,
    yet lived so long, master of her craft,

the goddess surely smiled on her.
But now Leira's gone,
do you really think our Lady
will offer the goddess
a bloodless girl of clay?"
Clio hugs this hearing
quiet and close as shame;
how can she tell her mother
what her best friend said—
that their vigil is all in vain
and no one else believes
Leira's statue may save their lives?

The moon fills up with a rush from one night to the next. One quarter left now, no more than seven days till its face shines full.

Clio takes Matti to the rising of the sun. Her mother is moving slowly this morning after another day of prising out rocks, but she lights a fire to cook barley cakes from their ration. She hates receiving rations like a slave, which feels quite different from the free choice of buying the same goods, but she's afraid of what will happen to food supplies if the raiders come.

And the truth is, if worrying about food distracts her from the terror of her daughter having only seven days left to live, she's going to concentrate as hard as she can on making these barley cakes.

Clio is thinking about food too. She knows her mother's feelings about rations, so as well as planning to pick as much wild artichoke and chicory as she can find, she's asked Mika to bring her a basket of fresh limpets, wrapped in seaweed to keep them cool. Mama's favorite.

Half-smiling about this, she bumps into Delia before she sees her.

Her friend turns, putting an arm out to steady herself and grabbing Clio's shoulder. "Who were you daydreaming of?' she asks.

Clio doesn't say, *My mother*, and she certainly doesn't say, *My horse*. "Can't tell you," she teases.

Delia pokes her in the ribs, harder than she needs to, though Clio thinks it's still friendly. "Am I seeing a tall herder?"

"Petros is just my friend!" Clio splutters—which makes Delia poke her again, giggling. She stays by her side as they move into the courtyard, so they're standing arm in arm, shoulders rubbing, as the Lady enters.

She can think whatever she likes as long as she's my friend again.

But in that moment, she feels Delia's body stiffen with tension. Clio looks up, and her own body mirrors it.

The Lady is mounting the wooden stage, in the east of the courtyard, as usual for the dawn ceremony. What isn't usual is that she's prepared for full ritual, with her face painted white as death, lips and cheeks red as blood. Gold snakes wreathe her arms and breast, and the red-flounced skirt, tight-laced bodice, and tall coned hat are the ceremonial costume that Grandmother Leira created on her clay priestess.

This is not the usual calling of the sun.

The prayer song is the same as every other day; the sun peeks over the mountain, the sky streaks with pink and gold—all the same as always, except that Clio's sure it's never taken quite so long before the sun finally shows his full golden face.

The Lady's song stops. No one moves; no one whispers.

Six priestesses step up onto the stage and flank the throne, as the Lady sits down instead of returning to the palace.

More ominously, the chief and six guards follow them. The chief is dressed in formal war uniform: leopard-hide kilt, bronze dagger at his waist, and gold bracelets on his arms; boar's tusk helmet on his head. He stands behind the throne and the others each step behind a priestess.

The other guards are scattered around the courtyard, with two at the palace door and four at the gate.

"Come close to the stage, my almost-women," says the Lady. Her voice changes to its oracle chant:

"The goddess calls you in desperate days.
Seven times more the sun will rise
before the rites
when the oracle will reveal
whether the Great Mother chooses
clay priestess or living girl.
No greater honor
than to serve the goddess,

to live with her in the after-life.
The chosen one will now live apart,
to rejoice and prepare
for the honor that comes."

"Everyone else leave now," the chief adds brusquely. "Praise the goddess and start your duties for the day."

In the close-packed courtyard, someone's breath warm on the nape of her neck, Matti's small body pressed against her thigh and Delia's hand in hers, Clio feels her heart freeze like winter ice.

The guards step into the crowd, herding them toward the gate. People push back, shouting and protesting.

"We need to be with them!" the mothers scream.

The Lady raises an imperious hand. "Let the mothers stay." The chief nods and the guards relent, allowing women to find their daughters.

Except Clio's mother, who's at home caring for the statue that was supposed to take her place.

The pain of it pierces Clio like a dagger. Delia's mother has an arm around her; every girl there has a woman's arms around her—an aunt or a grandmother if she doesn't have a mother. Only Clio walks toward the stage alone. Only Clio may never see her mother again, just like this, with no warning.

A new commotion at the gate, the guards booming, "By the Lady's orders: no one allowed in!"

A woman shouts back, her voice deep with fury and louder than the guards, "I will be with my daughter!"

"Mama!"

Selena, always afraid of saying the wrong thing, is screaming at the Palace guards. The world is turning upside down, but the part of Clio that is no older than Matti thinks, *I'm safe. Everything will be all right now Mama's here.*

The Lady raises her hand again. The guards stand aside and Selena races to Clio. "Fotia ran for me, as soon as the Lady spoke. She's with the statue now."

"Lady!" another brave woman shouts. "Our daughters are not prepared. Let us take them home and bathe them, dress them." *Bless them, caress them, say our own good-byes if we must.* The unspoken words thrum in the air.

Mama wraps an arm around Clio's shoulders and strokes her forehead.

"Times are dire," says the Lady, losing her oracle chant and back to her usual, elegantly commanding voice. Clio notices that her eyes are clear too, without the talking-to-the-goddess glaze. "The Great Mother has spoken and says that we do not have the normal time to prepare. The chosen girl will fast and cleanse before the spring rites, but there is no need for the others to stop work to prepare for the ballot. The goddess can see beyond grime."

Like the other mothers, Mama ignores this and tries to smooth the tangles from Clio's hair with her fingers, wiping smudges from her cheeks with spit, straightening her tunic.

"Before the ballot," the Lady continues, "the girls will pass by us, one by one."

The girls' ears don't hear and their legs don't obey; holding tight to their mothers, they shuffle around the court packed close together, more like a swarm of bees than the ant-file the Lady wants. Clio's crutch knocks someone's ankle and the girl cries as if she'd been slashed with a sword.

Two younger priestesses come to separate them from their mothers: "A procession," one explains, but a procession is for ceremonies, with clean hands and well-known rites—not for fourteen terrified and unprepared girls.

Finally, with the two priestesses herding like shepherd dogs, they file, weeping, past the throne and the watchful eyes of the Lady's entourage. The priestesses have seen all the girls before, because their mothers had presented them to the Lady at the new moon following their first bleeding. But now the girls must each give their names to the scribe priestess, who is seated on a stool at the far end of the stage with a basket of pottery fragments on one side and a tall necked pot on the other.

Will my piece be from our workshop? Clio wonders. *Will that be good luck or bad if it is?*

Great Mother, if you let me live, I promise I will do great things! Let me serve you as my grandmother served, above the earth with my own people. Goddess, my grandmother gave her life for this, willingly, serving you and our home the best way she knew how. I don't know what great thing I can do, but I pledge to find it. Just let me live…I don't want to die! No, no, no!

Felia is first. The scribe priestess marks her name on a pottery shard and drops it into the tall-necked pot. The next girl steps up.

But not everyone's name is written. At a nod from the Lady, the young priestess sends Baby Girl back to her mother.

Baby Girl's tongue is too big for her mouth; she's never had another name because she's never learned to talk and still cries like a baby. *Loved by the goddess*, the grandmothers say about children like that, deflecting their ill luck so it doesn't bounce on anyone else. Clio's surprised that her mother even brought her up to the Lady.

Then Sita, who stands, vibrant with health, head and shoulders above the other girls, is sent back. Clio barely has time to register this before it's her turn.

"Clio," she states, starting to step forward, so sure she'll be chosen that she forgets the ballot hasn't happened yet.

Delia gasps.

But we always knew it would be me, Clio wants to say. And can't, because the priestess is gesturing at her, not to her. Pointing her back to the waiting mothers. Rejecting her.

Clio hadn't thought she could be more numb than she already was. She was wrong. Now she's dead all over, removed from her body the way she learned to do when her pain was red hot and wanted to devour her. The scene on the stage is a long way away, as if she's watching through a haze of smoke.

Selena is weeping, stroking her daughter's face and head; Clio doesn't know if it's relief or shame, and Selena doesn't know either.

Ava, Petros's cousin with the crooked shoulder, is sent back too. Ten girls remain. They stand before the Lady's stage, waiting to hear the name, the fate, that will be pulled from the pot.

The scribe priestess holds it out to the Lady, who chants a prayer over it, asking the goddess to guide her in the choice. Or something like that—Clio's ears aren't working and she can't hear it. She's known the answer for so long she can't understand that it's changed; can't understand that her name isn't even there. She still knows it must be her, that her name will be called even though it isn't written.

"Delia," says the Lady.

Clio shrieks, "No!" as loud as Delia's mother. *That wasn't what I meant!*

Who did you mean, then? asks Leira's voice. *You knew someone was going to be chosen, and you asked for it not to be you.*

The silent scream,
*   When I said, "not me!"*
I didn't mean Delia instead—
I meant no one, no one at all
except the clay priestess—
and of all the prayers through my life
the goddess has never heard
why did she answer

the one I didn't say right?
Did Leira, who was priest-folk once,
    who talked to the gods
    and understood oracles,
    did she bequeath that god-gift
    when she died—
    Clio's never wanted power like that.
Never wanted to feel this shame—
    of being the one who triggered this
    by seeing the raider ship
    that made the Lady call the oracle,
    so that if there's to be
    a live-girl sacrifice,
    it should have been her.
Worse than that
    is if she had the power to speak to the goddess
    and by not knowing
    sacrificed her friend.
But the shameful worst of all
    is learning that she
    is a loved-by-the-goddess girl;
    she doesn't feel much loved at all.
She wants to live—
    doesn't want to die—
    but being too broken
    for the goddess to want
    is worse than being chosen.
Sita's bronze daggers
    are as fine as her father's—
    Doulos has traded them

around the world,
bringing honor to their land
and their goddess.
So strong and fierce she says she should
have been born a boy—
would Sita not have guarded
the goddess well?
And Great Mother, mistress of animals,
must surely love Ava's care of her goats
who she charms with her flute
and protects with her sling -
for though her right arm is stiff
she swings with her left
and Petros says
she is the best slinger of all the herders.
Even Baby Girl, strange as she is,
has a laugh that makes people smile
and clumsy kisses—
she doesn't simply cry like a baby
but rejoices like one too.
Clio doesn't
have skills like theirs—
but her crooked walk
honors the Mother no less
than before her crutch.
Like Sita's molten bronze,
fire flows through her,
glowing hot,
forcing her upright and strong,
her mind screaming,

Why should our blood be less
because of the fates
the gods have thrown us?
Even gods feel pain
though they cannot die—
do they not know
that every gift we give
is deepened by ours?
Are we not the same souls we were
before the fall
from a rock or a horse?
Now, though the Lady is chanting
the honor of serving the goddess
in after-life under the ground
and ecstatic priestesses lu-lu-lu,
pretending that Delia's mother wails
in celebration not despair,
Clio's screaming too—
the grief and horror of Delia's death—
and if she doesn't die,
how will she live
after these days of isolation,
neither priest nor slave—
a sacrificial beast
waiting for the knife?
A beast dies fast
but a girl must know—
Clio's grief swells again to rage—
at the raiders wanting what isn't theirs,
at the fates who spin their webs,

but most of all at the Lady
who made up her mind
not to wait for the rites as the oracle said,
but to waste Leira's death
and precious gift—
because Clio had seen by the Lady's eyes,
behind the white paint and kohl,
that the woman had decided,
not the goddess.
If the woman in her
can flout the Great Mother like that,
then I, says Clio,
an almost-woman
who prayed to be spared
because of the ways I could serve
above the earth,
must find my great things
and do them.
But now those short-tempered, short-memoried
guards
are shouting for everyone to leave,
get out of the court and back to work—
as if they've been idling at the well,
not driven here against their will.
Clio wants to hug Delia,
hold her for maybe the last time
but her friend is locked in a cloud of priestesses
disappearing into the palace
while the guards hold
her wailing mother back,

sweeping her like everyone else
out the courtyard entrance,
walling it off behind them,
looking like warriors
and not the men they know.
And though it seems a lifetime
since they held hands at dawn
the sun has barely risen—
as if he stopped his journey
to watch the drama
in their small town.
Please! Clio calls him,
silently, in her head,
if it makes you happy to see us working
outside in your light and warmth,
beg the Great Mother
to choose the clay priestess
and let Delia stay with us here.
She doesn't know what she has
to offer the sun
though she knows all gods demand
something in the end.
"Go," Mama tells her,
with a quick kiss on the forehead,
"find Matti
and take my place on the wall.
The raiders aren't coming today
and Delia's mother needs my help."
Sometimes Clio forgets
that Delia's mama and hers,

before they were masters of their craft
or mothers,
were heart-friends like Delia and her.
Though she remembers now
that when her sister, Matti's mother, died,
Delia's mama wept with hers,
bringing food and comfort
while they mourned.
So the guards say nothing
when Mama and Delia's aunt,
holding Delia's mother between them,
turn away down the street to her home.
Clio, still trapped in a bubble of ice,
shock deadening her legs
and a wall around her she can't break through,
trudges with the other not-wanted girls
and their mothers
out of the court to the street —
where Matti flies
like one of his stones from a herder's sling
into her arms,
hard head burrowing into her belly
and his clinging arms strong.
How could she forget him
even for that time,
abandon him without further thought
when called to the ballot —
the ballot with no use for her,
that declared her useless —
she'd left him in that

angry, roiling, excited mob,
without even calling
on someone to help.
"Where's Mama?" he shrieks,
    "I thought you weren't coming back!"
    He is hiccupping tears,
    his small warmth melting her ice.
"Who brought you here from the court?"
    Clio asks, and Matti stares
    because he'd simply grabbed a hand
    and the first he saw was Tail's;
    the silent carrier twin
    placed him on tall shoulders
    and took him to Aunt Hella.
"I saw Fotia running to your mama,"
    says Aunt Hella,
    appearing from nowhere,
    sidling close to ask,
    "To who the honor?"
"Delia," says Clio,
    which makes Hella sniff
    as if she
    could have directed the Lady better.
"Her mother will rejoice," she says,
    "for her daughter to bring
    such honor to the family."
If the raiders don't come
    and we're all still alive, thinks Clio—
    remembering Delia's burning eyes
    and her collapsing mother's shriek.

She wonders if Hella would feel the same
   if her granddaughters
   were not women grown.
"It was no choice of the oracle," she snaps
   hot and fast though to an elder.
   "The Lady wanted to be ready—
   but the oracle will choose on the day,
   when Grandmother Leira's statue
   is presented."
Just for a moment, before Hella turns away,
   Clio sees her squint,
   a flick of the eyes, clear as words:
   Aunt Hella is not of Leira's line
   and would rather pity Selena
   if Clio had been chosen
   than celebrate Leira's creation
   releasing a girl from death.

Clio is too numb to know where she's going. She can't
believe in Leira's prophecies now; seeing Mika and the
horses seems another betrayal of Delia. Easiest just to
trudge on toward the wall with the women rostered
there for the day, Matti clinging tight to her left leg.

Sita is ahead of her, walking fast, head raised
defiantly. Suddenly she is the only person that Clio
can bear to be with. Maybe she was stupid to think
that she'd be chosen—a limping girl with no particular
talent—but how could the goddess not want Sita, a girl
strong and perfect in body and mind?

Clio and Matti follow her into Igor's workshop.

Sita nods as if she was expecting her, and Clio sees that despite her defiant stance, the other girl's face is flushed with shame.

"My daughter!" booms Igor, grabbing her in his muscled arms and hugging her till even strong Sita is breathless. Igor lets her go and hugs Clio more gently. "It's good to see you safe too," he says. "Your family has given enough."

"But Delia…" says Clio.

Igor's face darkens. "Everyone has given enough," he agrees, his voice harsh and not as quiet as he thinks it is. "But there are better ways to serve—have you come to help my girl with the bellows?"

Clio knows he's joking, trying to lighten the anger. "Yes," she says.

Sita laughs bitterly. "We have some use, even if the Lady doesn't think so."

The smelting is done on the hottest of fires, the copper and tin melting together to form a whole new metal. Bronze is truly the gift of the gods, able to be cast in shapes of great beauty, galloping bulls or the acrobats that leap across their backs—like the potter's craft, the only limits are the artist's skill. But bronze can also be sharpened to a fine point on a spear head or a cutting edge on a sword.

The problem is that in all this great island, there is no copper or tin. When they have used what they have now, they will have to wait for the ships to return with new ingots that they've traded for with their cargo of pots, fabrics, and stone vases.

"Enough for another day or so," says Igor. "But none of it's any use if the fire isn't hot enough—get pumping!"

The bellows are goatskin bags, joined together to funnel air down the clay pipes that Delia had been so angry about making. Sita kneels behind the one on the left so that Clio's right leg has room to stretch behind hers. "Me—you!" Sita puffs, and they pump alternately, throwing all their weight onto their hands, Sita then Clio, Sita then Clio, on and on.

Matti leans against Clio's leg, chanting with Sita. The air puffs from the pipe into the heart of the fire. Flames flare; the coals glow deep, dark red, and as Igor shouts encouragement—to the girls, to the god of metals, to the metal itself, Clio's not sure—the copper and tin melt and mingle.

It's the hardest work she's ever done. It's all the punishment she could possibly want for not being on the ballot. She can't think of anything except keeping that rhythm—push, rest, forward and back, push, rest. There's no room to think of Delia, of sacrifices and fear, of being useless and rejected.

"Thank you," says Sita as they stand and straighten, stretching shoulders and aching backs. "It was good to do it together."

"But I still don't understand," says Clio, before she can stop herself. "Why wouldn't the goddess want you?"

"Because the goddess knows that though I have breasts and my blood flows each cycle with the crescent moon, part of me is more man than maid." Sita laughs, short and sharp. "And if that lets me stay alive I thank her for it. Serving may be an honor but I'm in no hurry to meet my death."

Mika doesn't see Clio all day. Petros isn't there either, though two new does and kids are in the enclosure. The fire is still warm in the hut; he must have left just before she arrived. She doesn't know if she should be in the hut without him; she doesn't know if she should be with the horses without Clio. But here she is, and she wants the warmth of the fire and the comfort of walls. She needs food too, though she'd never think of touching the drying cheeses, and she doesn't want to eat the limpets she gathered this morning for Clio's mother.

But strange as it feels to be alone here, she's grateful not to have to face her friends' eyes—not that Petros is her friend, and this morning is so bleak she's not even sure Clio is. Her mind darts like a fleeing hare but keeps coming back to admitting she doesn't want to see anyone. Doesn't want them to see that she's brought all her possessions—her goat hide that is both cloak and sleeping mat, the small stone knife she uses to pry limpets or oysters off rocks, her gathering basket, and wooden bowl.

Most importantly, she doesn't want anyone to see her face. Dymos has hit her before, has knocked her down before, but he's never punched her in the face the way he did last night. He hit so hard her head cracked against the ground, so hard that when she woke up she didn't know where she was.

She remembered quickly, and almost as quickly made up her mind. She was not staying with her brother for one more day. There was no point going to the other families for shelter; they had no room and telling him not to hit her again would only make him angrier. So she left, and she's never going back.

Did Dymos look as he stepped over her on his way to the sea that morning? Did he wonder if he'd killed her, and did he care? Or was it just her fear that he'd see she wasn't truly asleep, that made the step seem so long? She didn't know what she'd do if he started shouting again, started hitting again.

She just knew that he could never hit her enough to make her steal the horses.

It was Dymos who tried to steal them the night of the wild dogs! Mika had known it in her heart since Clio said the word "thieves", but she kept on hoping she was wrong. Hadn't quite believed that her brother, her only living family, could be so evil. The shock was another blow.

Not as hard a blow as the physical one. That had really hurt.

But she'd never have met Clio if Dymos hadn't chased Colti across the river. Wouldn't ever have learned to ride.

Except…will Clio still trust her if she tells the truth? Or Petros?

She doesn't know. All she can do is work it out,

moment by moment. To poke up the fire's warm ashes and add more sticks till the flames come to life. To watch the mother goats feed their newborns and watch the kids totter and then gambol on their miraculously strong new legs. To be very grateful that the goats out in the field are content in the corner where Petros has left them.

To whistle the horses to her, to stroke them all and groom Colti. Finally to bridle him, lead him to the mounting rock and climb on, to ride quietly around the field, wide around the goats to keep them inside an invisible fence in case they think of wandering farther. Which they will, no matter how content they seem, because they are goats. To stay on the horse as he grazes, lying back with her head on his rump, bending forward to stroke his neck, feeling the ripple of his muscles as he twitches off a fly, and knowing that whatever happens, she is right to choose the horses and defy her brother.

Petros returns in the afternoon as the sun is beginning to sink behind the distant western hills. Mika is so busy hiding her bruised face that at first she doesn't see his, which is bruised in another way. Not just exhausted, thinks Mika. Sad, grieving—and afraid. His voice is gruff when he demands, "Why are you still here? And without Clio!"

"I thought she was coming," says Mika, close to tears, because she's been so strong all day, brave on her own—imagining, planning, scheming what she's going to say when he comes, but now he's here, he's as hostile as when she first met him, the day after the wild dogs that turned out to be her brother. The day after his dog died, Clio told her later. *Has someone else died?* She is too afraid to ask.

Instead, gathering her courage, she comes out with the words she's rehearsed, even if her voice is a mouse's squeak.

"I cared for the horses as Clio would, and watched the goats so they didn't stray."

Petros acknowledges that with a nod, though his face is still tense. "Have they been to drink?"

"I was afraid they'd get away if I did it." She can't tell him of her terror of becoming a thief by mistake—what if she took the herd down to the river and couldn't bring them back? What if Dymos was waiting on the other side, still sure that she'd do as he ordered? "I could help you now."

"I've been herding since before you could walk—I don't need help!" Petros starts to snap, but stops. His sharp herder's eyes have just spotted the small bundle of possessions stowed near the corner of the hut. He adds it to the way she's trying to hide the black bruise radiating out from a swollen-shut eye...there's a lot the girl's not saying, but if she was ever a thief, she's changed sides now. He's sure of it.

And they do need the help. The palace doesn't know about her—she's not on any roster; maybe Clio's idea of having her become a herder isn't so crazy after all.

He picks up his flute to call the goats. "Whistle the horses," he says. "We'll take them to the river now."

Even walking up the valley path and seeing the horses safe near the herders' pen is not enough to lift Clio out of her haze of grief the next morning. But seeing Mika squatting by the fire with Petros, sipping milk from a bowl and wearing a herder's scarf around her tangled hair, is enough of a shock to wake her.

"I'm going to be a herder with Petros," the younger girl announces, so joyful after a night of warm, safe sleep that she forgets to hide her face.

Clio steps back in horror. "What happened?"

"I tripped and fell," says Mika. "Clumsy again!" Because that's what Dymos has always told her to say about her bruises. Even when their father and aunt were alive he would hit her when they were alone. She's been called "Clumsy Mika' so often that the word makes her feel sick in the stomach.

But you don't have to hear it anymore! says a small voice in her head. *You don't have to do what your brother tells you ever again.*

"Dymos wanted me to steal the horses for him. The night before I heard him talking to a man I didn't know—he said he'd win favor with the raiders with a gift that would turn the war. He thought if he kept hitting me I'd have to do it. But I never would! And I'm never going back. Never, never, never!"

"Will he try to find you?" asks Petros. "He'll guess you're here."

"You'll have to sleep at our house," says Clio. "He can't possibly know where we live."

Mika stares from one to the other. She hadn't

thought further than hiding in the herders' hut—she'd never imagined that Clio and Petros would look after her.

Her face drains suddenly, and she gasps, "He might…I don't know how—but I think he somehow knows where you live. I told him about the statue because I wanted him to understand that the horses were in a holy family, that could create a priestess to serve the gods. I wanted to scare him so he'd leave them alone. But he laughed, as if he knew something I didn't."

"Because your brother was the octopus fisher who came on the feast day," Clio says slowly. "He saw me carrying the statue. He laughed because he knows where to look for you."

"So she's safer here?" Petros suggests. "Even if I'm on the wall or lookout duty, the herd will alert her, and the old dog will protect her now he knows she belongs. Also, if you're going to be a herder, Mika, you need to learn to use a sling. You can have the one I've been making for Matti."

Clio doesn't hear. On the river road, when she was too deep in her fog to register anything, she'd seen a fisher, small and wiry as Mika, arms stained to the elbow with octopus ink.

"He was going up the road when I was coming down! I've got to warn Mama to say she doesn't know anything about you." She's already turning, her crutch swinging ahead as if it can't wait for her to keep up.

"He might hurt your Mama or Matti," Mika weeps. "And it's all my fault!"

"He won't!" Clio shouts over her shoulder. "Mama's not going to let anyone hurt Matti—and there are neighbors all around to help her."

Of course the neighbors aren't all around at the moment, they're out working on the wall—but Granny Pouli is there, right across the road, she reminds herself. Granny mightn't be able to move but her curses would terrify the bravest warrior. Mika's brother is just a bully who beats up his little sister.

Clio's moved fast with her crutch before but she's never run. This is running. Breathless, panting, up-the-hill running, her crutch with a life of its own, dragging her leg along, every part of her focused on reaching home before Mika's brother does. She rushes past a palace washing girl so fast she nearly knocks the linen out of her arms.

She can't get there before him, it's impossible—but can he really know where they live? Did he actually see her going into the house after the procession? She'd been concentrating so hard on not dropping the statue that she'd barely noticed him. Why did Mika have to tell him about the statue—was she trying to betray them after all?

No. If Mika had wanted to betray them she'd have helped him steal the horses like he wanted. She told him about the statue because she wanted to impress him, to frighten him, to make him stop beating her—*just like I told her all about the statue, let her see the*

shrine, simply to impress her. No one was beating me.
Would I be as brave as Mika if it happened to me?

But what if Mika's right—what if he hits Mama to make her tell where Mika is? So much chaos in the town, would anyone hear her scream? What if he hits Matti?

The thought of that makes her go even faster. She didn't think it was possible. She's at the gate.

"What's your rush?" asks the guard. "Why aren't you on a work party?"

"A fisher!" Clio pants. "Did a fisher go in?"

"This isn't the time for chasing pretty fishers!" he mocks. "And that one's gone out again, if it's the one I'm thinking of. Now get back to what you should be doing!"

Out again. He's had plenty of time for Mama to tell him where Clio meets Mika. Plenty of time to bully it out of her if she didn't give it at first.

Clio tries to force herself to calm, to breathe, not to knock people's legs in her rush.

The sound of wailing as she turns onto her street— Selena's voice from the winemaker's house; neighbors running, calling for Granny Pouli's granddaughter.

Clio's own home is empty. Completely empty.

The statue is gone.

Her mind can't believe
    what her eyes say is true—
    Leira's statue disappeared.
Then the lu-lu-luing tells her:
    Granny Pouli has died;

Selena has taken the priestess
to watch over the death.
Spinning into the street
and straight into Mama
"Granny Pouli has gone to the goddess—
I heard her cursing the raiders,
the chief, the Lady and the fates—
then a groan that made me run—
the gods had stopped her heart.
"I'll take the statue
to oversee the passage,
beg a little mercy for a woman so old—
and with this initiation, as if of a priestess
hope the Great Mother will see that this clay
serves better than blood."
Then Selena, seeing it gone,
screams as if for another death—
as it is, for the oracle now
has nothing to pronounce
and Delia's dying is assured.
"Mika's brother!" Clio wails.
"He tried to force her to steal
horses for the raiders—
now he's taken the statue instead—
if only I hadn't gone to the field!"
"If I hadn't gone to Granny!"
her mother wails in reply—
"but there was death in that groan
and how could the goddess forgive
leaving an old one to make that journey alone?"

But they know he can't have gone far;
    the guards are so angry,
    so ready to fight,
    they can surely capture him
    before he gives the Mother's servant
    to the raiders who worship
    the angry sea god.
Racing together to the gate,
    Selena trying to explain—
    a traitor has stolen a statue of power
    to bring down the town.
The guards shift their weight,
    foot to foot like anxious horses—
    more afraid of offending the palace
    than a potter losing a statue
    whatever the value.
"If it wasn't in the temple
    consecrated by the Lady
    it has no power," says the old tall guard—
    they don't seem to care that without it
    Delia will die.
So while Selena argues,
    Clio slips past—
    Mika will know her brother's ways,
    where he'll go or how he'll hide—
    and whatever her beginnings
    Mika's no thief now.
Clio longs
    to catch the traitor any way she can—
    if she was a slinger

she'd bring him down
with one swift stone—
but she doesn't have a sling
or know how to use it
and she can't run.
She curses the fates that let him arrive
in that short blink of time
with Selena just across the street
while she was on the hill.
Down the river road—
though her fastest now
is slower than going up—
onto the goat path to the hut,
knowing every moment
takes the thief farther away.
Mika has the horses groomed,
Fleet Foot and Fouli locked in the pen
so they can't follow,
Colti bridled and the chariot out—
"I don't know how to harness," she says,
"but I've rubbed her down
and told her you're coming—
horses are faster than a man on foot—
may the gods all curse
the man who used to be my brother."
"I'd go if I could," says Petros
but I'm rostered for the wall today
and they'll search me out if I'm not there."
"Mama is trying to send the guards,"
but Clio's harnessing as she speaks—

the guards have waited too long
to catch one man who knows the land.
Leira's prophecy becoming clear—
it's never safe to mock the gods
and the Lady had promised
the oracle a choice—
whatever she might have chosen
rage at a promise not kept
means Delia will die,
and all in vain
as the waiting raiders
are called in by vengeful gods.
So now,
without guards or weapons
with nothing but their fiercest rage
it's up to Clio and Mika
to save a girl's life.

CHAPTER 11
FACING THE TRAITOR

Emotions war inside Clio, between wanting to go as fast and soon as they can, and knowing that driving the chariot still isn't natural for her. She needs to rehearse every step in her mind, hearing Hector's voice as she does it—because if Gray Girl panics, if the chariot breaks or she falls out, they'll never catch Dymos or save the statue. So she tries to ignore the thumping of her heart and the clenching in her belly; concentrates on tightening the harness straps; on not jerking the reins when she drops the crutch into the spear strap and slides her bottom onto the woven leather seat. Her strong left leg slides onto the board as she gets into place, and she hoists the right one beside it.

Mika leads Colti to the mounting rock and climbs onto his back.

Take a breath, Clio tells herself. *Lift the reins and*

tell Gray Girl to move on. Just like the practices; just like when we herded the goats.

Fouli squeals, rushing at the fence. Gray Girl turns and neighs for him. Clio's not going to be able to control the mare if she keeps wanting to go back for her foal.

"Will I let him out?" Petros calls, opening the gate. Fouli gallops to his mother, and this time she moves on happily when Clio clucks. But it's not a good start.

Not much more than a moon ago she'd dreamed of crossing the bridge and following the road toward Tarmara. Now that it's happening it's more like a demon-dream. Gray Girl trots over the bridge, Fouli at her side; Colti and Mika are a little way behind. The colt is still wary of the bouncing chariot's creaks and rattles, but only hesitates a moment before crossing too.

On the other side of the bridge, the shrubby wildness near the river quickly becomes close-grazed goat field. Mika takes Colti into it so she can ride beside the chariot, only pulling back onto the road where the field becomes too rocky to be safe.

Clio's palms are so wet with sweat she has to keep wiping them on her tunic so they don't slip off the reins. But she's concentrating so hard on the driving, on keeping an eye on Mika and Colti in case he bolts or she falls, and another eye on Fouli in case he lags behind, that for a moment she can't remember why.

Only for a moment. As if she's not exactly forgetting but resting.

"I can't believe we're doing this," Mika exclaims. "It doesn't seem real."

The bumping, lurching chariot, the thumping of her bottom on the seat and her legs on their board, the feel of the reins in her hands—that's all real. The scent of oregano where Colti has trodden on it; the salt sea air blowing in from the north, the cooling breeze on their faces—all real too. Concentrate on that.

Because chasing a man who's stolen Grandmother Leira's statue, a traitor who is Mika's brother; racing to save Delia and the town…that doesn't seem real.

"Where will he go?" Clio asks.

"I don't know. But if we don't catch him, he could make it to the raiders' winter camp by dark."

Suddenly, Mika gasps—so loudly that Colti startles and hops. The girl nearly falls; grabs his mane to pull herself back on. "Sorry, Colti, wonderful horse," she says, soothing and stroking his neck. "Thank you for letting me ride; I won't scare you again."

Carefully keeping her voice level, she says, "Dymos might take the boat if he gets to our place."

"I thought you didn't have a boat!"

"Our uncle does."

"Would he loan it to him?"

"No. The family worships that boat like a god, because it gives them power over the rest of us. They'd never let him take it."

"But he's already stolen a sacred statue," Clio finishes for her. "Why wouldn't he steal a boat?"

"I heard him tell that man he didn't want to be a

fisher all his life. He said he could be as good a warrior as any of the raiders."

Fear squeezes Clio's throat; she opens her mouth three times before any words come out. Even though she's seen him and knows he's a man, she's always thought of Dymos as Mika's brother and a boy. A traitor, a thief, a wicked boy—but not a warrior. The very word makes her shudder. She's been so intent on catching up to him that she hasn't thought of exactly how they'll get the statue back. She'd thought her rage and doing the goddess's work would be enough.

It doesn't seem enough to face a warrior.

She doesn't even have a whip to protect them. Hector said that a whip was useful for many things, not for beating but to touch the horse's side as a guide, like a longer arm. But he hadn't had time to make one before he left—and he'd never imagined she'd do enough driving to need it before he returned. *He didn't imagine I'd be driving at all before he returned*, Clio thinks. But right now it would have been comforting to have a weapon.

"We need a plan."

Clio's mind whirls. "Will he stay on the road to your home? Is there another way?"

"Only the beach, if he thought the guards were chasing him."

"They should be!" Clio snaps, turning to look back down the road one last time. She knows the guards won't follow unless the palace orders it, and the Lady can't order it if she doesn't know about the theft.

Would she even then? Or is she so sure that the oracle will ask for the sacrifice of a real girl that she wouldn't bother?

Feeling her girl's fear, Gray Girl tosses her head. The chariot lurches. "Sorry," Clio calls, just as Mika had to Colti when she squealed.

"So he'll go by road till he hears us following," she concludes.

"If he knows it's us, he'll stay on the road because he won't care. But if he thinks it's the guards he'll run down to the shore."

"Did he have his spear when you saw him?" Mika asks suddenly.

Clio tries to picture the man she'd seen. *Why didn't I pay attention? Why didn't I know that was important, instead of being so lost in grief I've caused more?*

She'd noticed his ink-stained arms…she'd have seen a spear. And the guards wouldn't have let a stranger into the town with a spear, even a fishing spear.

"No spear," she decides.

But they still don't have a plan. If they go faster he'll hear them sooner, but if they go slower he's got more time to hide and get away.

The road curves around a hill, taking them close to the clifftop. It's a long drop down to the beach. The hill is thickly wooded but becomes goat pasture again a little way ahead.

There's a man on the road. Too far away to see who it is, but the way he turns at the sound of the hooves… "It's him!" Mika hisses.

There's no time to think. "Come on," Clio calls to Gray Girl, lifting the reins, and the mare responds as if Clio was riding and had squeezed with her knees. Her trot is smooth as a lullaby, Hector always says, though the little chariot jolts and lurches behind it.

Mika only hesitates for a heartbeat—or maybe Mika doesn't get a choice, because Colti doesn't want to be left behind. He's right at their side, too close, way too close—there's no room on either side of this road. "Pass us or get behind!" Clio shouts.

A blur of dark horse and ashen-faced girl flies past them. "Use your legs!" Clio shouts. "Sit up and pull him back!"

"I'm trying!" Mika shrieks.

Gray Girl's racing now too; the chariot bucks along the road, bouncing Clio hard on the woven seat and slamming her legs onto their board. She's tugging on the reins, harder than she ever knew she would, and the mare's not even slowing—the real race is whether Clio and the chariot flip over before Mika falls off Colti. The colt and rider are well ahead now, closing in on the man standing in the middle of the road.

Why doesn't he move? Isn't he afraid of being run over? The horses would never trample him on purpose, but it's what people are always afraid of.

They're past the forested hill; the goat field on the left is open and bare.

"Turn into the field!" Clio shouts to Mika. "Circle back to me!"

Mika doesn't seem to hear. The colt has his neck out and head up; it's a miracle that the girl's stayed on his back. Her brother is still in the middle of the road, refusing to move—and the colt's turning. Looping a wide, wide circle into the field and up the slope of the hill, which slows him enough that she can turn him back toward Clio.

Gray Girl, now that Colti's not ahead of her, finally slows too.

They're close enough to see Mika's brother's face, though that's not what Clio's looking at. He's holding the statue high in his left hand, and in his right, his trident fishing spear.

The spear is wooden, long and thin. The three ends are black, hardened by long smoking in a fire and ground to such fine sharp points that they look just as lethal as the palace guards' bronze spearheads.

Of course he didn't try to take it into town—he hid it to pick up on his way back. How far would those prongs sink into a horse's chest?

Clio yanks Gray Girl back, hard and sharp. The mare comes to a full halt.

So does Colti. Mika flies over his head. She somersaults as she hits the ground, taking barely a moment to catch her breath and jump to her feet—but never lets go of the reins.

Clio watches out of the corner of her eye. She doesn't dare look away from Dymos. How far he can throw that spear? Ten paces? Twenty? They're fifty paces apart now and it seems much too close. It feels as if he's trapped Mika and Clio instead of the other way around, and if they blink he'll move fast enough to spear one of them, horses or humans.

Dymos laughs, a short, nasty sneer. "Not even the horse wants you, little sister. This is your last chance to get on the winning side. Come home now and I won't sell you to the raiders. If not you'll have to watch me spear the horses—and take your friend into slavery with you."

"It's a fishing spear," Mika murmurs to Clio, though her voice is shaking. "He's never killed so much as a rabbit with it on land."

Her voice carries farther than she wants.

"Never had such a big target," her brother calls, laughing again. "Even that little one is too big to miss! Come closer, baby horse—come and see my spear!"

He's stolen the clay priestess, he's threatening to kill the horses, to sell his own sister and me as slaves—and he makes it sound like it's all a game.

Like copper and tin merging to become the stronger new metal of bronze, fear and anger boil together in Clio—her body cramping, sweating, her fingers like ice and hot heart pounding. But when she opens her mouth, what erupts is a whole new strength.

"You touch that foal and his mother will trample you before you can flee! You'll kill nothing and sell no one as a slave!" she roars. "Give us the statue now to take to the temple where she belongs!"

And then Mika, her left arm still holding Colti's reins, uncoils the rope sling looped over her shoulder and takes a stone from her pouch. Petros had given them to her with one very quick lesson while Clio was running back to town. She wouldn't dare try it so close to the horses but Dymos doesn't know that.

"You don't know how to use that!" he scoffs, but his voice isn't quite so sure. This is a sister he's never seen before.

"I didn't know how to ride a horse a moon ago," says Mika, her voice strengthening and deepening into a shout. "A day ago I hadn't said that you will never beat me again, never order me again—and that I will never, ever go home! Do you dare believe I won't use this sling and stone against you?"

"Goddess hear us," Clio screams in echo, and Granny Pouli's curse-chant gushes out of her mouth.

"First your eyes and then your teeth
one by one your limbs grow weak.
To atone the ill luck made
Gods demand a high price paid:
Fear will spread its deathly pall
and into slavery you will fall."

She can feel the power as it leaves her and hits him. For a full ten heartbeats Dymos stands still, trapped by her words.

Then he shakes himself, like a dog shedding water. "Why should I give anything to the goddess who's given nothing to me?" he asks bitterly. "Why should I care for a town that mocks and stones me, that brought my grandmother into the world as a slave for the stinking drudgery of the purple? She was freed by the one god-hearted person in that miserable town, but she never lost the scars of body and soul from those early days."

"And you'd sell me to the same life?" demands Mika, her face scarlet with fury.

Dymos doesn't get a chance to answer before Clio shouts, "That god-hearted person was my grandmother! Leira the potter, priestess of the Swallow Clan, who escaped her island before the Battle of the Gods, became a purple slave before escaping to become a potter. A potter who worked to save the life of every slave she could, your grandmother and many, many like her. Would you destroy this statue, created with the last breaths of her life to save more lives?"

"Your grandmother?" Dymos asks Clio. "Truly?"

"By the Great Mother's eyes," Clio swears, "Leira of the swallows was my grandmother."

Dymos stares at her for the length of a lark's song, his face twisting with the pain of decision.

He's going to try to spear us anyway; he's going to take the statue and run; he's going to throw it against a rock and smash it...

"Give it to me," Mika says firmly, tossing Colti's reins to Clio and stepping toward her brother.

He hands her the statue.

Mika passes it to Clio as quickly as she can, and takes back Colti's reins.

Clio checks it quickly. It's unharmed but how is she going to drive and hold it? This precious, fragile object that must be perfect, not a finger or ringlet chipped, or the oracle will reject it just as surely as the Lady had rejected Clio herself.

"Your herders' scarf!"

Mika unwinds the long yellow headscarf. Clio wraps the statue in it and then ties it around herself like a mother carrying a swaddled babe. Mika checks that it's tight, then, in one smooth movement, leaps back onto Colti's back as if she's been doing it all her life. They start toward the town.

Dymos doesn't call after them. Clio turns once and sees that he is still standing motionless in the road. It's too far to make out his face but his body shouts of despair. *Could he be sorry? Mika's evil brother—could he be ashamed of all that he's done?*

"Is he following us?" Mika doesn't want to look. She refuses to see her brother again.

"No," says Clio. "You're safe."

Mika doesn't feel safe. She feels shivery and empty, as if her life spirit has floated away from her body.

"Grip with your legs!" Clio says sharply, seeing that the girl is about to slide right off the horse. "Colti needs you to guide him."

Mika tries. She feels the warmth of the horse's body under her, the friction of his sweaty coat, the solid strength of the neck as she twines her fingers through his wiry mane. Slowly, the life spirit flows back into her; her energy returns.

But the way home seems much, much longer than the way out.

Clio can't look back, can't wonder
    whether Dymos will change his mind,
    whether Mika will fall,
    if the oracle will accept the statue
    or if their chase has been in vain.
    All she can see is the road
    and her only task is to drive it.
So close to the cliffs
    the air is fresh with the salt of sea;
    farther up in the hills
    sheep are bleating;
    birds chirping their morning song
    as if this is any spring day;
    a cuckoo calls, the first of the season,
    so close and clear
    the horses toss their heads.
Clio risks a glance behind—
    the empty road doesn't calm
    her fears as it should.
    When Mika rides up beside her
    looking strong again—
    "Let's trot!" calls Clio.
  "Don't wait if I fall," says Mika.
    "Colti will always follow Gray Girl home."
She's brave, this girl, thinks Clio,

but I can't leave her here
and the statue is safer
the slower we go.
"We'll walk," she says,
    and though Gray Girl is ready for home,
    wanting to quicken her step,
    Clio holds her back
    to move more smoothly down the road.
Past the wooded hill,
    round a bend to face the sea—
    the glimmering bay so close
    she thinks they might run over the cliff—
    she doesn't remember this stretch on the way—
    but the road curves again, sending them east,
    looking up to the hills
    where the town nestles and Leira is buried.
Now the snake of the river
    the shrub of its banks,
    still in the distance
    but the road straight to the bridge—
    Fouli races ahead to drink—
    Clio sees in her mind
    the chariot toppling,
    stuck in the river or drowning—
    she steers Gray Girl on over the bridge—
    and though Colti swerves to the bank
    Mika clings
    to his back like a burr
    and is safe.
Gray Girl smells home;

trots off the bridge, straight into a canter
up the river road;
veering to turn down her path
but obeying the touch of reins and voice,
keeps on toward the town,
Clio bouncing and rattled,
hair blown to a tangle
wind-tears in her eyes
and her grandmother's priestess
riding every step and bounce
safe on her chest—
she is as one with her horse
as in the days she could ride.
Now it seems that the mare
knows as well as Clio
where to go and what to do—
if Delia must wait for the oracle
inside the palace,
so the clay priestess must too.
The Leira voice clear in her head...
The priestess will come as priest-folk must,
not from a workshop of humble craft
but with the symbols of power and glory—
the god-spirit of beasts—
to take her to her rightful place
at the Great Mother's side
having vanquished those who would harm her.

Palace guards are at the gate. They are wearing their
armor, bronze breast plates, helmets and greaves; their

spears and huge shields are leaning against the gate posts behind them. They don't know Clio as the usual guards do, and they are not smiling.

A messenger has brought news, Clio guesses. News of the raiders. A chill goes through her.

She reins Gray Girl in hard and can hear Colti stop behind her, Mika murmuring to him—she didn't fall off! A flash of pride in her friend makes her braver.

"Clio the potter, daughter of Selena, granddaughter of Leira of the Swallow Clan—I carry the clay priestess that the Lady needs for the spring festival oracle."

The older guard raises an eyebrow and points to Mika.

"She helped me recapture the statue," says Clio. She doesn't mention that it was Mika's brother who'd stolen it.

"With the horses?" he asks.

"With the horses," Clio repeats, her heart thudding. She's suddenly very sure that's exactly what the Leira message means—the Lady must see the horses.

The guard laughs. "Go!" he says. Both guards step aside, and the horses trot through the gate, down the street to the palace. Their hooves ring on the cobblestones; the chariot bounces, but the clay priestess is still snug against Clio's chest.

Even with so many people out working on the wall, the street is noisier and closer than the horses have ever seen. Their ears are flat back; they toss their heads and swish their tails. The townfolk leap out of the way— they barely recognize the chariot driver as Clio and have never before seen the wild-eyed girl on the back of the other horse. Rumors have been flying around the town all morning—are these girls an advance party of raiders?

"Call the guards! How did they get past the gate?"

"It's Clio, you children of fools!" bellows Igor the Bronze. "In the chariot Hector built her! Let them pass."

Muttering, the crowd draws back. But at the courtyard entrance, more guards jump to block them.

The horses roll their eyes in panic; Colti is sidestepping. Clio hopes he doesn't kick.

"Keep back!" she shouts.

"You don't give orders!" a guard bellows back. "Why have you brought these beasts here?"

"I bring the clay priestess for the oracle!"

The enormity of what she's doing swamps her. The Lady told Grandmother Leira that the statue must stay with them until the day of the oracle. How can Clio dare to defy her?

How can she dare not to, when she's been ordered by her own oracle, her own dead grandmother?

Then the Lady herself calls, in that clear voice that never sounds like a shout but carries to every corner of the courtyard, "Step away from the horses. Let the girl through with the offering."

Clio looks up. The Lady, in a fine red bodice and flounced skirt, is on the balcony above the court where she announces the oracle's decisions. A priestess stands on either side of her, as if this truly is an announcement from the gods.

The girl, she said, not the horses. Clio thinks she should get out—but she's so nervous that she inadvertently lifts the reins when she reaches for her crutch. Gray Girl walks quietly forward into the court. Fouli and Colti aren't going to be left behind; the foal is tucked so tight against his mother's side that the chariot struts are digging into him, and the colt is following close behind. Clio doesn't think Mika could hold him back now and is glad she's not trying.

They stop in front of the balcony. Transferring both reins to her left hand, Clio places her right hand over her heart—and over the clay priestess strapped to her chest.

"Your grandmother was Leira of the Swallow Clan?"

"Yes, Lady."

"And you have the statue she created as an offering for the spring rites?"

"Yes, Lady."

"That I ordered should stay in your home, with the vigil of a newborn, until the day when the oracle would decide if the goddess would accept this gift in the place of a living girl."

"Yes, Lady." Clio's voice trembles, but she never drops her gaze from the Lady's face.

The Lady stares back, the distance between them becoming nothing as she looks deep into Clio's eyes as if searching out her soul. Finally the Lady draws a deep, shuddering breath.

"Your grandmother is wise, in death as in life. You

have kept faithful vigil over this statue for more than the required moon's cycle. It is right that it should be brought to the goddess now, in the same way the flesh-and-blood girl has."

That flesh-and-blood girl is Delia! Is she watching from a window, the way she may watch from the underworld later? And couldn't I see her, just for a moment?

"Thank you, Lady," she says.

A heartbeat later, the palace door opens and the young priestess who'd herded the girls the day of the ballot approaches the chariot.

"I will take the statue to the Lady."

Clio freezes. She can't undo the statue's tightly knotted sling with one hand and Gray Girl is much too twitchy to let the reins go. She glances at Mika, who's struggling to keep Colti under control.

"Turn to the side," says Selena, as calmly as if she's combing out a knot in her daughter's hair at home. Clio hadn't even seen her arrive.

So Clio turns, and her mother leans over the side of the chariot, unties the knot at her waist and gently takes the swaddled statue from the scarf.

"Go with the goddess," Selena murmurs to it. "We give you our prayers, our hopes and our dreams. Live with the Great Mother and keep us safe."

Just as gently and reverently, the young priestess receives it. She returns to the palace. Now only the goddess can decide what will happen.

Clio knows she should feel relieved—she's honored

the oracle's demands, and now she and Selena won't have to juggle their time to keep vigil.

She feels bereft, as if she's lost someone she loved.

But there's no time for reflection, because the Lady is speaking from her balcony again.

"I thank you, daughter and granddaughter of Leira of the Swallow Clan. But who is this girl on the black horse? She is new to our town."

"This is Mika," says Selena, hesitating because she doesn't know Mika's mother's or grandmother's names, and Mika doesn't seem to know that she should tell them.

"She is our new apprentice," says Selena, "from a fishing settlement toward the west."

The Lady's face is motionless, but Clio senses she's not pleased. She calls up all her courage again.

"Lady," she says, "Mika is a child of no learning who's known little love, but she has braved great dangers to rescue the statue from one who would have taken it to the raiders' camp."

The Lady is silent for a long, long moment, staring into Mika's face the way she had into Clio's earlier. "Our town needs courage at this time," she says at last. "We thank you, child."

Leaving the horses, watered and groomed,
   for Mika to watch with the flock —
   hoping the herd behaves
   for the pale and shaking girl —
   the road home has never been so long —
   Clio so pale and shaky too

the guards don't ask
    why she's not on a work party now.
The house empty with the statue gone—
    easy to join the wailing
    for Granny Pouli's death—
    but there's one thing more Clio must do,
    Selena too:
    "We must tell Leira her statue is safe,
    where it belongs," they say together.
"I'm coming too," says Matti,
    "and so is Goatie."
In a basket, Selena carries
    three feast cups
    and a small jug of ale,
    barley cakes, and cheese
    from Petros's hut.
Matti carries his wooden goat
    and Clio nothing but her crutch
    and heavy heart.
At the graveside they offer
    libations from each cup of ale,
    share barley cakes upon the grass,
    and sing the statue's tale
    for Leira to hear.
Matti tells her
    of the clay balls he's made,
    of offering them to the guards
    who jeered and told him to find more stones;
    of how Petros said
    the balls shoot farther and better than any rock

and is making Matti his own sling in thanks—
Clio doesn't tell him
the first has gone to Mika.
While Matti chatters,
  galloping Goatie around the grave,
  and Selena sings a song for the dead,
  Clio is lost in despair
  for now the horses have rescued the statue,
  Leira's oracle words
  have been fulfilled—
  and although she rejoices
  that Mika's training and her own
  were all to gain that noble end—
  she can see no more purpose
  for her horses or for her—
  "I'll do my best with the clay," she vows—
  but her heart is empty.
Sudden and strong, the Leira voice speaks:
  Clay for the head—
  the heart may follow in its time—
  but your work is greater
  and not yet done.
  Find the power within,
  not tamed by pain or loss of limb—
  the god-spirit in the horses
  is no greater than that in you.
  Grow your strength and skill
  to match that power—
  give up now and you risk
  the lives of all.

CHAPTER 12
PIRATES

Hector is at the tiller, steering the swallow-painted ship out of a great trading port. Doulos is resting in the small cabin after last night's celebrations. The Lady was right: they've done well by starting the trading season early. They've already traded nearly half their goods, with more profit than ever before, including thirty-two ingots of good tin. Now they have a last long sail across to the Island of Copper before they return home, laden with everything the town needs to make the precious bronze.

Ahead of them, their sister ship has already hoisted her big square sail. But as they clear the shelter of the port and Hector calls for the oars to be shipped, he dreams of pushing the steering paddle farther around and ordering the sailors to keep on rowing toward home. Five more days till the full moon of the spring festival. He would give up all the world's bronze for the chance to see his daughter before then; to ignore the Lady, the oracle, and the gods themselves to rescue her, fleeing across the island in the chariot he'd built with such love and care.

He can't. He doesn't. It's a dream that never leaves him, but with each day it's less relevant—he doesn't know if they could possibly make it in time now. No one sails against the winds to go that way around the trading route.

Suddenly he sees it, an eyeblink before the lookout in the bow shouts the warning.

A sleek, black-hulled raiders' ship.

Pirates.

They've come out from behind a rocky islet. Their sail is up, filled and fast with the strong north wind.

"Row!" shouts Hector. "Into the lee of the island!"

The islet's steep cliffs will block the wind; the pirates' sail will be no use. They'll both have to depend on their oars.

The men pull hard, but the ship is heavy. The pirates have time to pick up their own oars and chase them.

Doulos staggers out from the cabin, rubbing his eyes, as Hector shouts, "Turn port NOW!"

The rowers lift their starboard oars out of the water, haul hard on the port, and turn the ship toward the shelter of the island.

The pirates do the same.

The long sharp snout of the pirate boat rams the swallow-painted ship. Doulos staggers and falls; rowers tumble from benches; Hector shoves the tiller with all his strength—but the steering paddle doesn't move. The ship is hard against the rocky cliffs of the little island. Water is pouring through the hole in the side.

Cheering wildly, the pirates pull out daggers. Before they have even loosened their sail, the first rowers are scrambling over their bow to leap onto the swallow ship's deck. Hector reaches for his dagger. "Fight, men!" he shouts, running down the center bridge to haul his brother-in-law to his feet. Doulos is staggering, a trickle of blood running down his forehead, but he waves his dagger fiercely.

A gust of wind, a whirling whim of the god of the sea, fills the pirates' sail.

A messenger arrives from a village outside Tarmara—the raiders are readying their ships. Rumor says they're coming to Gournia first.

The raiders that Mika's brother would have given the clay priestess to! thinks Clio. *Thank the goddess she's safe with the Lady.*

It's the only good thought in a world of fear.

There's no rest, no excuses, for work on the wall, except for a new task of hauling water from the well to vats at the gate and along the walls, in case the raiders try to set fire to the town.

Clio grabs a big water pitcher and heads to the well. She can only take one jug at a time and it's not much lighter work than digging out rocks, but it might be an easier one to slip away from. The only thing she knows for sure is that she must obey her grandmother's oracle voice, even if it means disobeying the guards.

The town crackles with anxious laughs and bad temper. There are mutterings about Delia being chosen without proper ceremony, and more mutterings about the guards who don't seem to do any work except for ordering everyone else to do it. They've ordered so many to haul water that there's a line of five women and girls at the well when Clio gets there.

"The palace servants won't be working this hard to get buckets to every door," someone mutters, because the palace has water that runs in pipes to wherever they want it.

Is Delia carrying water buckets through the palace like a slave? Or lying in a bath with warm and scented water like a priestess?

Two guards are at the entrance to the palace courtyard, maneuvering a giant pithos, taller than their heads, into position beside another four already filled with water.

"I'll fill it," Clio volunteers.

The guards are stretching and rubbing their lower backs. The older one nods and Clio steps toward the palace, her pitcher in her hand.

"From the town well!" bellows a senior guard, stepping in front of her so fast he nearly breaks the jug. "Do you think the Lady and her priestesses can be interrupted by craft-folk wandering around the palace?"

Can you see me, Delia? Are you watching from a window?

"Go!" the guard barks.

It takes all morning to fill the pithos. She never sees Delia.

The crowd is a tangle of tinder, ready to explode. Dogs pick up the tension and walk around the streets snarling and snapping. A boy guard runs past with a bloody nose.

"He got off lightly," says Igor the Bronze, but Clio never hears why.

A stone vase apprentice bumps a weaver's pitcher as she leans toward the well. The weaver slaps her.

"Does it matter who fills the pithos first?" Sita snaps. "Let the girl go ahead and thank the goddess for another moment's rest!"

The weaver huffs. Clio's so shocked she nearly drops her own jug. She can't believe anyone her age would speak to an elder like that.

But Sita just shrugs. "We'll have as much fighting as we want if the raiders come. No need to start between ourselves."

The weaver shouts about respect; everyone is too busy arguing to notice when Clio slips home, her right arm shaking with strain and left armpit chafing from leaning so hard on the crutch.

Selena is at the winemakers, helping to prepare Granny Pouli for her funeral. Without hesitating in her farewell song, she crosses the road to her daughter and starts to massage her shoulders.

Matti darts in from the workshop, carrying a basket heavy with clay sling stones. "Are you going to the horses now? I need to take these to Petros."

Clio is so weary she wishes she could stay with the mourners and sing for Granny Pouli. But her grandmother's oracle words were clear, her mother's shoulder rub ends with a little push that says, "Go!"— and perhaps Matti is telling the truth that Petros wants these clay stones.

"Let's go," she says.

The horses are with the goats in the river field, and Mika is watching them from Colti. She looks so at one with the horse that Clio is stabbed with jealousy all over again. Gray Girl has been a part of her life—a part of her—for as long as she can remember, but she'll never again share a moment of relaxed comfort like that.

The mare trots up, nuzzling her face with velvety lips that say she loves her girl, no matter where she is.

Mika waves and turns Colti toward them.

"Where's Petros?" asks Matti.

"Wall building," says Mika.

"But I need to give him these stones!"

"More clay balls!" Mika exclaims. "He says all the herders should have them to fight..."

"...to fight bad dogs," Clio interrupts. Even though Matti knows he's been collecting stones in case of raiders, she wants to protect him from thinking about what that actually means.

Mika looks surprised. Clio guesses that no one has ever protected her from any terrible news. But the girl understands quickly and adds, "You can leave them here and he'll see them tonight."

"If I can't practice with Petros," Matti says, following Clio to the hut, "can I ride in the chariot with you?"

"Yes," says Clio, "that's exactly what I need to practice today."

His excitement has invigorated her—and it's a big enough challenge that she won't be able to think about anything else. Not Delia or raiders or whether Dada will come home safe. Maybe that's why she's so sure it's what she needs to do.

The little boy stands behind her in the chariot seat, his hands on her shoulders and his head next to hers, peeking over one side then the other. They go twice around the goat enclosure, then down the hill to cross the bridge. Matti's small body is warm against hers, and by the time they trot back up the path, she's as relaxed as if she was on Gray Girl's back instead of driving behind it.

Matti relaxes too. For the first time, while Clio is unharnessing, he goes willingly to offer freshly plucked grass to Fleet Foot. The filly allows him to stroke her face as she nibbles and steps around him, grazing placidly when she's finished.

"When I'm big," says Matti, "I can ride Fleet Foot like Mika and drive a chariot like you."

Clio ignores the stab of pain; doesn't shout, "I used to ride like Mika—I was the one who taught her!"

"Yes," she says. "You can do both, goddess willing." *If we're not both dead or slaves by then!*

Four days till the full moon. Three. Two.

Granny Pouli is buried. The west wall is nearly built. The giant pots of water are filled. Selena and Clio have baked barley cakes with all their remaining barley. Matti has delivered more baskets of baked clay balls to Petros, and Petros has shared them with his friends. Clio has practiced driving every day with Gray Girl; Mika spends the days on Colti. Petros's sister's baby has seen a full cycle of the moon; Petros's mother has started going up to the herder's hut to make the cheeses when Petros is on lookout or wall duty.

There is more news of the raiders and their preparations, but still no sight of them.

> Waiting so long
>   for this doom to come,
>   it weighs heavier every day
>   like a black cloud pressing,
>   like the ash that covered Leira's home—
>   except the ash was real
>   and this is not yet—
>   they are still alive,
>   still free, still breathing—
>   just very, very afraid.
> Working is not enough
>   to keep fear away;
>   laughter might, for a fleeting moment—
>   but all laughter is gone,
>   a distant memory from last week.

Everywhere, people are clumsy
   as never before
   tripping over Clio's crutch
   and their neighbor's feet.
Even the carrier twins
   with a load of spearheads, the last of the bronze:
   Head lowered his poles
   but Tail didn't—
   the twins who always moved as one
   moved as two
   and spilled the spears.
Ever since that proof
   that the world is wrong
   Clio's felt a rumbling hum,
   a whirr of bees in her belly
   as if the fear is running itself,
   making sure she won't forget
   for one blink of an eye
   that it's always there
   and there are many reasons for it.

Suddenly it's the last day: the spring festival, with all its
rites and sacrifice, is tomorrow. News speeds around
the town—although the Great Mother's decision won't
be announced till dawn, the Lady will read the oracle
tonight, when the full moon rises.

   Selena doesn't care what the guards order—Delia's
mother needs her. She walks away from her work on
the wall to find her friend, knowing that if she's not
at the grave of ancestors she'll be in front of her own

house shrine. Clio pries out a final rock and follows, detouring home first to fill a basket with figs, cheese, and barley cakes.

Delia's grandmother is rocking and moaning in a corner of the room. Delia's mother's cheeks are streaked with tears, but she and Selena are singing to the house goddess, hands on hearts and their voices clear and strong. Clio enters quietly, needing to be there and wondering if they want her: *do they blame me for the oracle, or for not being the sacrifice?*

Selena welcomes Clio with her eyes and nods toward the kitchen; Clio puts her offerings onto a platter and watered ale in a cup.

The thought of food makes her feel sick, but she offers the cup to Delia's mama, who tips a few drops of ale onto the floor for the goddess before passing it to her own mother. The old woman stops to gulp a great mouthful—and when she hands the cup to Mama, picks up the song with the other two women as if she's never hesitated. So does Clio, because honoring the goddess seems like the most important thing she can do at the moment.

They sing through the entire chant in front of the house shrine, like the three ages of women in a rite: the maiden, representing the one who may be lost, the two mothers, and the crone.

Sometimes Clio wishes that Leira could have created the statue and stayed alive, but it's impossible even as a wish. The clay figure couldn't be the powerful creation it is, worthy to take the part of a living girl, if her grandmother hadn't breathed her own life into it. Now, the day the choice will be made, Clio understands as she never has before.

So when she has sung, and choked a piece of barley cake down her dry throat, she goes home. Matti is out collecting stones with the other children; she is completely alone in the house. Exactly as she needs to be.

A small mound of clay, wrapped in wet reeds and ready to use, is in the corner of the workshop. Clio doesn't want to attract the guards' attention by sitting outside at her wheel; she carries a lump inside and sits with it on the clean stone floor.

Knead and smooth, knead and roll; the clay is cool under her palms, soothing as she digs her hands in deeper, squishes more firmly. Knead and smooth, knead and roll…long ropes of snakes, as if she's going to make a coil pot, but she's not. She doesn't know what she's making but it's not a pot.

With closed eyes she lets her hands do what they want, rolling the snakes back into a ball and starting again, the soft clay yielding and resisting and forming into something new, something that has never been created before. There is no time; no place outside this small world of herself and the clay.

"Oh, my daughter," says a quiet voice, "granddaughter of Leira. It seems you are a potter after all."

"Did Clio make that?" Matti demands. "All by herself? Is it a friend for Goatie?"

Clio wakes from her trance. It's evening and the

room is dark. A small clay horse is between her hands.

The clay is for the head, the voice said, *but the heart may follow.*

I thought you were telling me my path was with the real horses—not a clay one!

Complete your task with the living beasts and you may yet choose—one or the other, or a new way of both. Fail and choices will not be yours.

Her mother places the clay horse reverently on the drying rack. "Come," she says, "the moon is rising."

Over the east wall, over the mountain, the moon hangs low, huge and gold, as if it waits near the earth to see tomorrow's offerings.

They stand in the street with their neighbors, lit by the unearthly shadows. Clio thinks she'll scream if anyone mentions that the Lady must be reading the oracle now, or speculates on what it will say.

No one speaks.

Clio is awake long before dawn; Selena's breathing says that she is too. Clio drags her sleeping mat closer and nestles her head on her mother's shoulder.

"Whatever happens is the will of the gods," says Selena, gently stroking her daughter's hair. "The Great Mother meant you to see the ship that day."

"But if I'd put the figures into the kiln myself..."

"I've thought long on that, and so did my mother. It's a rule that should never be broken. But she believed—as does your father, and so do I, though I was slower to come to it—that the call you felt came from the goddess, and a call from the gods is above all other rules. You did what was laid down for you."

"But Delia's paying the price!"

"It's the goddess who'll decide," says her mother, though there's a quaver in her voice. "We must remember it's an honor."

They sing a quiet prayer to the little house goddess—Clio wonders if she feels alone now that the clay priestess has gone—and wake Matti to eat an early breakfast of lentil porridge with yogurt from the goats. Once the sun rises there'll be no food again till sunset, which reminds Clio of Mika's brother trying to sell octopus at the last fast day. Is he still plotting harm to the town? She shouldn't have trusted him just because he'd given the statue back. What if he comes after Mika again? What if…

"You told the Lady of the traitor," Selena says. "It's in the gods' hands now."

Clio hadn't even realized that she'd been worrying aloud.

"Can we go yet?" asks Matti.

They'd laid out their clothes before they went to bed: Selena's long brown wool skirt and yellow-dyed bodice; Clio still in the tunic of childhood, because she won't be given her woman's skirt for another half year, on the autumn full moon day after light and dark are equal again. But it's her good cream wool tunic, freshly washed, and so is Matti's, and they all wear their jewellery—Matti a single strand of clay beads around his wrist and the amulet around his neck, but Selena and Clio with bead headbands in their hair as well.

Matti's shaved head is stubbled now; Selena smooths it with a few drops of olive oil. She wears her own simply tied at the back, because she is passing into old age, but arranges Clio's in as elaborate style as is allowed for a craft-folk nearly-woman, a high ponytail with ringlets at the side.

They're the first ones out in their street, but when they reach the palace court, in the faintest glimmer of gray morning light, Delia's family is already there. The two groups huddle close under the balcony where the Lady will proclaim the decision.

"She'll have to sing the sun first," Delia's mother moans, as the courtyard fills behind them. "I don't know if I can wait so long to hear."

Torches flare from the dark balcony, and the Lady appears in front of them, white-painted face gleaming eerily. The oldest priestess stands on one side, holding the statue, with Delia on the other. Delia's face gleams nearly as white and eerie as the Lady's. She is limp and ghostlike; in the flickering torchlight they can glimpse the young priestess supporting her from behind.

Clio can't breathe. It feels as if the whole audience is holding their breath.

"Let the people see the choices," the Lady says at last. The priestess lifts the clay statue higher. Delia steps forward — then sways and disappears from sight.

Her mother sways too. Selena catches her, wrapping an arm around her waist. Around them, people breathe out in muffled sobs and sighs.

When the Lady comes down to the courtyard to call the sun, her song is clear though her eyes are still oracle-glazed. But Clio can barely focus on the stage; her eyes keep wandering to the palace door. Delia's mother is as close to it as the guards allow.

Delia doesn't appear. Not even when the sun has risen free of the mountain and the courtyard is being prepared for the sacrifices. Priestesses chant and dance, while musicians shake rattles and pound drums. There's not much room for the townfolk to dance; their turn will come later, when they go out to the streets and fields; for now they sing and sway around the edges.

The sacrifices are led in; a heifer calf, a ram, and a goat, their heads wreathed with flowers. One by one, to songs of their beauty and power, they are taken to the altar stone. The chief slices their throats with his sharp bronze knife; the Lady catches the blood in a golden bowl, then a bowl of bronze and one of fine porcelain.

Finally the priestesses dance to the palace door and reappear with Delia. She wears a fine white tunic flowing to her ankles; her hair hangs in long, loose ringlets and her head is wreathed with flowers like the other sacrifices. She is carrying the clay priestess.

The audience gasps like a single person. *Not both!* Clio screams silently. *Goddess, no!*

Delia's eyes are glazed; she sways as she walks. Two priestesses guide her to the offering stone, where she sits, still holding the statue.

The Lady's voice is deep as she begins to chant.

"Times of great need
call for great gifts,
sacrifice from all.
The Great Mother demands
a server for all time —
blood for life,
wisdom of age,
beauty forever.
We give her fresh beauty
created with the blood
and wisdom of age —
a server priestlike as a god,
bringing grace to our need;
leaving the girl to become
a woman grown,
serving in her best way —
returning to life
as the sun climbs the sky
on this great day of balance
between light and dark."

The oldest priestess hands her the golden bowl, brimming with blood. The Lady turns to the offering stone and pours the blood over both statue and girl.

Then she takes the blood-stained statue from Delia,

still sitting stunned on the stone, and lifts it high, to east, north, south and west.

"Goddess hear us; accept our gift of a priestess to serve you forever and bring us peace and plenty in the coming year."

The courtyard erupts into joy, singing and laughter. Delia's mother breaks free of her friends' supporting arms and races to embrace her daughter—blood-soaked, dazed, and alive.

They are still rejoicing when the cry comes from the watch guard, racing breathless through the streets from Watchtower Hill.

"Ships! Ships in the bay!"

"Dada!" shrieks Matti.

But these aren't Dada's ships. There are two sleek black-hulled ships, and the speed they're moving at means that these are warships, not traders. Without enough breeze for sails, they are skimming across the bay. No one needs to see the oars, or the shields along the sides—they're easy enough to imagine. In the same way, Clio knows that one of them is the ship she saw in winter, that day a lifetime ago, before the oracle, before the statue, before Grandmother Leira died.

The crowd goes instantly from joy to pandemonium. Parents scream for children to flee for home; guards shout indistinguishable commands; men run to collect weapons and dogs bark at the fear they can't fight.

Clio clutches Matti against her right hip—somehow they've been separated from Selena in the rush—the little boy is heavy to carry but he's already crying and there's such a press of people she's afraid he'll be trampled. Her crutch hits legs, tangles with the stick of a one-legged weaver and they all nearly fall.

Selena, struggling toward them against the flow, hands back the weaver's stick and grabs Matti from Clio's arms.

"Delia's mother is taking her to her brother's mountain herding hut—we should follow them."

Already the first people to run home have packed babies and belongings into packs on their backs and are fleeing to the hills, to huts and caves.

Clio knows it would be sensible. They're a girl with a crutch, a grandmother, and a not quite four-year-old child. They have no skills to fight off warriors.

"Take Matti," she says. "I need to stay with the horses. I don't know what I have to do, but I need to be with them and I think Mika does too.

"Then we'll stay with you," says Selena. "Petros's hut is close enough to run to, but not easy to see from the road."

Quickly, Selena tells the house goddess what's happening. She explains that the best way they can honor her is to hide her. Clio climbs the ladder to the upstairs sleeping room and rolls the little figurine into a pile of bedding, with an offering of honeycomb to allay the insult.

There aren't many other valuables to hide. They put the small pots and vases in baskets and store them in a big kitchen pot as if they were going to be shipped. The ones that don't fit are tucked under shelves. Matti e their offerings out to the fields. Because if the town rvives this day, they'll need the goddess's blessing for e coming season. So the Lady offers a bowl of blood the olive trees, and cuts the first stalks of barley with er small silver sickle.

Usually the procession takes all day, with the whole opulation chanting and singing their way around the ields. Fires roasting the sacrificed beasts feed the gods with plumes of scented smoke, leaving the meat to be eaten as soon as the sun sets. Everyone would dance through the town and the fields, as late into the night as they can stand; the feast cups that Selena and Clio have prepared would be filled with watered wine or ale, enjoyed all night, and smashed at the end.

Not this day.

The Lady and the priestesses return to the palace as soon as the offerings are made. The streets are even more frantic now. As well as the mothers and grandmothers fleeing with babies on their chests and packs on their backs, young farmers and herders are heading into town. They carry their family's spring offerings—a lamb or kid, a bag of grain or wine—but nothing else except their scythes and axes or staffs and slings. They have come to defend the town while their families take the herds to safety. Fishers stream in from the harbor, where the raiders are likely to land. Like the women fleeing to the hills, they have their children and whatever possessions they can carry. Dogs sense the fear in the air; they snarl at newcomers and their dogs; the animals brought in

buries Goatie under a pile of soft cla
the cooking fire is out. Selena gives (

Her mother's knife! Clio stares ;
It's no longer a tool she borrows fc
branches—it's Mama's own defense.

"Take it!" Selena says gruffly.

"But…"

"Take it," her mother repeats, and C
cold and heavy in her hand. It makes
demon-dream real. Warriors are coming ;
smash the homes, steal all there is to take
the townfolk or capture them for slaves.

Could I use this to cut another human
meat but never killed it. Never even killed

Matti is crying again because now that h
Goatie, he wants it back. Selena unburies it fo
he rocks it like a baby.

Now Clio knows she could use the weap
red power of rage ripples through her; she's ;
than she's ever been, bigger than she is—nc
going to hurt Matti.

Or Selena. Her mother who's given her thi:
instead of keeping it for herself.

Or the horses—although she's suddenly surc
she's misunderstood the Leira voice. There's no
that two girls and two horses can save a town or ;
a war.

That's the Great Mother's job—and now the pal
guards are bellowing, shoving, clearing a way throu
the chaotic streets for the Lady and her priestesses

for sacrifice bellow and bleat. Every baby in town is crying at once.

But the ships don't turn. They continue on across the bay, past the point where they would angle in toward the town; a west wind has sprung up and their filled sails are pushing them steadily farther away.

"Praise the Great Mother!" people sing in the streets. "We're saved!"

"They're heading to Moklos," cries a fisher. "Goddess save our sister town!"

Selena replaces the house goddess on the home shrine. "But I'm not unpacking anything else," she says. Even the food and jug of ale for tomorrow stay in the basket packed for a flight to the herders' hut. Matti gallops Goatie around the empty floor. Clio feels awkward, disconnected. She can't see Delia; they can't work, but it doesn't feel like a feast day.

A gong sounds to call everyone to the court. The chief appears, backed by four palace guards. They are all bright with bronze, as if the enemy is still close. The chief climbs onto the stage, and the tallest guard bangs his spear against his shield. The silence is immediate.

"I have prayed to the gods of war. The ships have passed us by for now, but to defeat them we must go to the aid of our sister town." The chief looks around, checking that everyone's still paying attention. They are.

"It's true that our enemy has two ships of warriors. It's true that each of those sixty fighting men is well armed and shielded in bronze. But these barbarians, who would attack on a sacred day, do not have the blessing of the gods. I will lead the guards to defeat them as they think to destroy our sister town."

A murmur of discontent and fear runs through the audience. The chief raises an imperious hand. "We will not leave Moklos to burn—and we will not leave the raiders victorious to slaughter us when they're finished with our sister town. The four palace guards will remain with the Lady. Sing your praises loud to the Great Mother that she continues to protect us—and obey the Lady's commands in all things, as she obeys the goddess. This is how we save our town."

Then the chief and fifteen guards, with their helmets of bronze or tusk-covered leather, their swords, spears, and tall wooden shields, march briskly down the road that winds past the purple works and on to Moklos on the eastern side of the bay.

Clio and her mother watch them out of sight. "Matti and I will stay here to honor the Lady's rites," says Selena.

"I'll go to the horses," says Clio. Her mother nods and kisses her on the forehead. "Take the knife," she reminds her. "The ships have passed, but who knows what evil this day will bring."

Mika is whistling the horses when a figure appears on the goat track. Petros has just left to bring the does with newborn kids into the pen, before his mother and sister lead the herd up to the higher mountains.

Several have strayed deep into the valley, out of sight from the hut.

The fear in her belly tells Mika who it is long before she can see his face.

She thinks of hiding; thinks of running. Instead she whistles again. She would rather face any danger from Colti's back—and that includes her brother. The other horses won't go near enough to a stranger that he could hurt them.

Through the cold fear, she feels a thrill of power when Colti trots to her—and although she's still afraid of Dymos, she's glad that he's seen it.

The bridle is already in her hand; she'd groomed the horses at dawn, singing her own type of prayer for whatever was happening in the town, for Clio's friend and the statue that her brother had tried to steal. She doesn't understand it all, but she knows that Clio is worried. Mika wants Clio to be happy even more than she wants the town to be safe.

Colti accepts the bridle easily; she leads him to the mounting rock. Jumping on from the ground doesn't always work as smoothly as it did the last time she faced her brother, and she's not going to risk falling in front of him. He's close enough now that there's no doubt it's him.

"Get out of here!" she shouts. "The herder's close by and he'll bring you down with a rock from his sling if you try any harm!"

Dymos shows her his empty hands. He's out of breath, panting as if he's been running.

"Raiders are coming!"

"We've already seen the ships—and they've gone past anyway."

"There's a land army too."

"You're lying."

"I'm not! They're going to attack the town while the ships take Moklos."

"Why would you tell us? How do you even know?"

Her brother looks down, avoiding her eye. "I took octopus to the camp two days ago. I heard the talk— the land army would attack here the morning the ships sailed across the bay. They'll have the whole coast."

"You're just trying to scare me into going home."

"There's no home left."

Mika stares, open mouthed.

"They attacked yesterday. It was just practice for them; sport. Our uncle is dead; everyone else has been taken as slaves. I was diving—they didn't see me. You have to warn them."

"Warn who?" demands Clio. They were so intent that they didn't hear her coming. "What are you threatening?"

"Not threatening," says Dymos, and tells his story again.

Suddenly Mika believes him. So does Clio.

"You have to tell the Lady. The guards have left to help Moklos."

"She won't believe me," Dymos says bitterly.

"We'll go together," says Clio. Her mind races. She wishes she could approach the palace in her chariot again, but the streets are chaotic, and by the time she harnesses Gray Girl, it won't be much faster. They'll have to walk.

Mika is thinking the same thing, jumping down from Colti and removing his bridle. She's glad she mounted to meet her brother—she feels much smaller without the horse.

But not as small as before I ran away!

She runs to catch up with Clio, who's already started down the hill.

They see the smoke as they come up the river road. North-east across the bay, the direction the raiders were heading—their sister town is burning, the town they trade and share skills with, exchanges that lead to marriages and families intermingling.

The fire must be huge. This is not a spring festival bonfire; it's not one house or olive oil press: it's every pithos of oil in the town; every house and villa and temple. And if they're all burning like that, what has happened—is happening—to the people?

In the still-blue sky high above them, vultures wheel, and wing their way toward the smoke.

The guards bar their way to the palace courtyard. The Lady is visible from the open balcony doors, singing to the goddess at the upstairs shrine, and cannot be disturbed by two girls and a skinny, ink-stained fisher.

"Please," says Clio. "We have news of the raiders."

The guard glances at Dymos.

"I saw them myself," says Dymos.

The guard still hesitates.

"Lady!" Clio shouts, louder than she knew she could. "A land army comes!"

The Lady's hymn trails gracefully to a close and she comes to the balcony. "Who says this?"

Dymos steps forward.

"The traitor who stole the priestess statue?"

She's looking at Mika, who nods, unable to speak. The Lady turns her gaze to Dymos. "Why should I believe you?"

"Because I came to tell you knowing that you might drive me away, or worse."

"Let them in," says the Lady.

They are ushered across the court to a room on the ground floor. The Lady seats herself on the wooden throne and listens intently to what Dymos has to say. Her white-painted face can't grow paler, but her mouth becomes rigid with tension.

"We must send word to the chief and the guards," she murmurs, almost to herself. "We need them back. Guard! Who is our fastest messenger?"

"Lady," Clio interrupts hesitantly, "a horse is faster than any man."

"You can follow with your chariot?"

"Not as fast as a single horse and rider. Mika—"

"Can you do this, girl? You will follow the road to Moklos to find the chief. You will tell him that I bid them return, for we are being attacked by land. Then you will ride back ahead of them and bring me the news."

Mika nods. She can hardly breathe; she has no idea where she's going and can't imagine giving orders to the chief—but deep inside, she's more exhilarated than afraid.

"You can speak, can't you, girl? Repeat the orders back to me!"

Mika does it. The Lady nods, and takes a ring off her right hand, telling the young priestess to tie it around Mika's neck with a cord. "Show this to the chief and he will know that you've come from me. Now go, quickly!"

They turn to run. "But you, granddaughter of Leira," the Lady calls after her, "return when the girl is on her way. I may have other need of you."

"And the traitor?" asks the guard.

"Keep him under your eye. If he's truly no traitor, he'll be glad to join in the fight to defend our town."

At the herder's hut, Petros's sister, her sleeping baby strapped to her chest, has just started to lead the goats up the mountain. His mother is packing the last of the cheeses into packs on two big billy goats' backs.

"Will you bring the horses and come with us?" she asks.

"The Lady has need of them." Quickly, while Mika bridles Colti, they tell her the news. She kisses their foreheads and hands Mika a skin bag of yogurt. "You have a great task, and you're no use to either Lady or gods if you collapse before evening." Then, with a sheepskin cloak round her shoulders, a rope sling and pouch of stones at her waist, flute at her throat, and staff in her hand, she taps the old dog and is gone, up to the mountains that are too wild and steep for raiders to follow.

Then Mika is gone too, trotting Colti down the track to the river road.

> Horse and girl move as one,
>   a long smooth trot
>   from hut to river road,
>   faster up to town,
>   turning onto the road to the sea
>   with barely a pressure
>   of the girl's rein and knee,
>   as if thought is enough.
> The road straight between olives and barley
>   to shipsheds and fishers
>   on the shore of the deep blue bay—
>   Mika has never been so far—
>   a quick fear flashes
>   that they'll land in the sea—
>   but the road forks above the beach
>   and they veer to the track on the eastern coast,
>   following the chief and his guards,
>   hoping they're not too late
>   to save the town.
> Colti moves into a canter
>   where the track is smooth,
>   the joy of his gait says she could ride forever
>   and they'll be in time—

when they're struck by a stench
like a blast from a gale,
a stink of rotting, putrid fish,
making Mika gasp
and Colti spin to flee—
Mika's new fear now
is she'll never stop him till he's home again;
failing to find the guards,
failing the town
and her only friend.
Weeping, pleading,
wrestling the horse with knees and reins
she calls on the gods—
the god of horses,
though what does he care
for the fate of a town if the horses are safe?
So she calls on the goddess that Clio worships,
Great Mother of all.
A sudden silence—
the wind whispers soft,
salt scent of sea lifting the stench;
Colti turns to her touch;
the girl loosens the reins in relief—
the horse takes the bit between his teeth
and bolts.
Mika doesn't call
on the gods again.
Through the squawking of gulls
she hears a laugh
as if the goddess is saying,

"I've turned the horse—
it's up to you to stay on."
She can barely try to rein him in,
can do nothing but cling—
if she falls
there'll be no message at all—
so her thighs clamp
and though her right hand
tugs hard on the reins
the left grips tight to the flowing mane.
Perhaps the horse
is truly driven by gods
for he stays on the track,
flying past the purple works—
the stink and clamor,
following the curve of the bay,
the track sheltered by trees
at the foot of rugged hills.
And though the chief and the guards
are far ahead
the horse and girl
are gaining fast.
Slowing on a steeper hill
emerging from the screening trees
to the top of a cliff
where a black-hulled ship
sails so close to the point
Mika thinks if she leaned out,
over Colti's ears,
she could spit on its deck.

As the sail is furled and the oars splash out
    she feels the eye of the tillerman
    direct on hers—
    a strange and fear-filled moment,
    for a girl on a horse
    can mean nothing to a pirate
    though a raider ship
    means everything to the girl.
The ship clearly headed now
    straight to Gournia, her new home—
    and no one knows
    except her.
If she follows her mission
    to call back the guards
    no one will warn the town
    that the raider ship comes—
    but if she doesn't tell the chief
    there'll be no guards
    returning to help.
Mika stares at the ship,
    stares back down the road
    and up ahead
    to where smoke still rises
    from a hidden, burning town—
    when she sees ahead,
    sun glinting on bronze,
    the chief and his marching guards.
Colti still breathing hard
    starts into his trot
    around a curve and down a slope

then canters up,
hooves thundering on hard track
so the chief and guards turn
and Mika faces
a thicket of spears.
"Halt!" shouts the chief—
as if the spears didn't say enough.
"I come from the Lady!" Mika shouts back—
Colti obeys her reins and stops.
Mika lifts the Lady's ring
from around her neck,
delivers her message word for word—
raiders coming by land,
the town needs chief and guards to return.
"And you, girl," says the chief as they start,
"Follow far behind us, or flee to the hills—
this battle will be
no place for a child."
"But Chief," says Mika,
heart beating fast at her nerve—
"from the cliff I saw
a raider's ship
rowing hard toward the town."
At a glance from the chief
a young guard runs
through the trees to the cliff—
"It's true!" he shouts.
"A black-hulled ship
on its way to our home."
"Ride!" says the chief to Mika.

"Tell the Lady we follow
as fast as we can—
but with land army on one side
and a ship on the other
the Lady herself
must flee the town."

CHAPTER 13
THE PURPLE SLAVES

Clio doesn't know how long she spends staring after Mika and Colti. The black jealousy worm chews at her heart again as she locks Gray Girl, Fouli, and Fleet Foot into the enclosure around the hut so they'll be easy to catch. She tries not to wonder if she'll be here to catch them.

It doesn't matter that she knows how dangerous Mika's mission is—Clio's trained all her life for a ride like this and the destiny should have been hers. Now she'll never know if she'd have had the courage to do it.

Your tasks are not done, says the Leira voice in her head. *Leave the child to hers so you may serve as you must. Return to the Lady as she commands—you will give her more than she knows to ask.*

There are more of the purple than those who wear it; a vast army is hers if she opens her eyes. But to fight for a homeland they must belong, not as sheep or goats but human souls.

Tell the Lady this. If she understands, the Great Mother will smile.

"How do I give oracle words to the Lady?" Clio demands.

Grandmother Leira's ever-young voice disappears and Clio is alone again.

But the Lady has told her to return. She didn't mention the horse, but over and over, Leira's oracle voice has insisted on Clio practicing with her chariot. There's only one way she can go to the palace.

Numbly, she cleans the chariot with the rabbit-hide polishing rag, grooms Gray Girl again, soothing herself as much as the horse, and harnesses her. She leaves Fouli locked in the enclosure with Fleet Foot. He squeals shrilly; Gray Girl whickers back and then walks on.

"Thank you, sweet mare," says Clio.

The sentries at the gate seem to be expecting her. "Make way for the horse!" the older one shouts down the street. Clio holds the reins firmly, expecting the mare to be as skittish as she'd been the first time she came to town, but Gray Girl is calm. They drive through the empty streets to the crowded courtyard, where the old and ill, babes and tots huddle in fear, watched over by the four palace guards. They're the tallest of all the guards, armed with spears and daggers, great shields at the ready; only the chief himself could be armored more. They meet Clio at the entrance and motion Gray Girl through, one guard ahead and one trailing the chariot.

The Lady is waiting on her stage, still in her bright layered skirt—but over her blouse is a guard's bronze and leather jerkin, and instead of a peaked ceremonial cap, a bronze helmet sits on her flowing hair.

"Approach," says the Lady. "The guard will hold the horse."

Clio takes her crutch from its holder and alights as gracefully as she can, patting Gray Girl on the neck. "Stand still for the guard!" she whispers. The mare flicks an ear in reply—Clio hopes it means "yes".

"When I told to you return," says the Lady, "I didn't command the horse and chariot. The goddess tells me now they have a part in what is to come. But how did you know?"

The Lady is not someone to lie to. "The voice of my grandmother—she's been telling me to train with my horses since my father left on the ships."

"Did she have any other word for today?"

Clio takes a deep breath and chants Leira's message.

"There are more of the purple
than those who wear it;
a vast army is hers
if she opens her eyes.
But to fight for a homeland
they must belong—
not as sheep or goats
but human souls."

"The purple slaves," the Lady says slowly. "As your grandmother was once, I believe."

"She told me," says Clio, "that she'd been priest-folk, slave, and master of her craft, and though the jobs were different, her soul was always the same."

"And now, from the grave, she directs me to free them. To make them human."

"She would say, Lady, that they are human now, but that we should recognize them as that."

"And I say," says the Lady, "that as a land army comes from the west—we have had another messenger confirm it—and the ships that burned Moklos come from the east, our town needs help from everyone to survive. You will take me to the purple works now."

"I'll take you?" Clio repeats, too shocked to be polite. The Lady travels in a palanquin chair carried by two guards. That's how it's been since the world began. "How?"

"In your chariot!" the Lady commands impatiently. "Why else have you learned to drive it?"

The priestesses and guards look even more anxious than Clio. The Lady ignores them all. She steps down from the stage, crosses to the chariot and steps into it, standing at the back and holding a side rail with each hand.

She frowns as Clio places the crutch in its stand.

"Lady," says Clio, fear drying her throat so she can hardly speak, "I need it to walk—and there could be a reason we need to get out."

She waits for the command—not to argue, to throw

it out—but the Lady calls for the young priestess to bring her a scarf, bright with priestly purple, and ties it to the crutch like a flag.

Clio slides carefully into place in front of her, not daring to touch the folds of the regal flounced skirt. Her heart thumps, and she breathes deep to steady it. Then she lifts her reins and clucks. Gray Girl walks on through the courtyard and down the street, the four palace guards following close behind.

Through the gate, down the road to the sea, past the olive grove and field of barley—the grain ready to cut, if it's still theirs and standing at the end of the day—to the rise above the beach where the road forks; the fishers' village to the west and the purple works east.

Clio has never been to the purple works. Despite seeing the slaves when they deliver broken shells, or the few that her grandmother was able to buy to freedom, the place itself has always seemed like a myth. Now the stench floats closer, more real than she's ever wanted to imagine. Gray Girl snorts and skitters in the traces; Clio keeps a steady hand on the reins and soothes with her voice, though she's not sure whether she should be talking to the mare in front of the Lady.

"The horse has its place in this work," says the Lady, reading her thoughts. "Speak to her as you always would."

It's still not easy, especially as her quiet words are drowned out by the clanging of rocks and hammers, cries and curses. The Lady tells the scar-faced guard and the one who limps to go ahead and command the slaves to assemble at the front gate.

The silence is immediate. The space fills with scrawny, half naked people: children, women and men, all filthy and blotched with purple, all terrified.

"Move forward," says the Lady to Clio. She coughs slightly but makes no other sign that she can smell the terrible stink. "We'll stop at the rise."

They face the assembled slaves, the Lady standing behind Clio, the two tallest guards at Gray Girl's head, and the other two on either side of the chariot. Clio watches as if she's floating above the scene; she sees her own hands sending calm through the reins, feels the mare shudder once and then settle.

"People of the purple," the Lady begins, "we thank you for your work on the wall. Your lives are hard and you have not been appreciated as you should; as human souls."

The listening slaves show no response. Thanks and appreciation aren't words they've heard before.

"Today an army comes to attack us by land. The smoke you have seen is from our sister town, and the ships that burned it hope to return here to do the same. The chief and the guards have gone to the aid of this town and may not be back in time to help us.

"But we will not be defeated, for we have brave hearts in the town and the fields around—and in you. Come to fight with us, and when we are victorious you will no longer be slaves."

The silent disbelief is loud as a shout. One brave woman cries, "Where will we live, Lady, and how will we eat, if we are no longer at the purple?"

"You may work, live and be fed here as before, but you will be as free to travel or change tasks as any other craft. You'll be allowed into town. There is little shelter here against the raiders; those who are too young or weak to fight may go to the town now, to be protected with the other folk.

"It will not be easy, neither the fight nor the victory," she continues. "But you can take heart from the stories of Leira of the Swallow Clan, who was a slave here and became a master potter, and of the many people she took to freedom. Have the courage to fight and the rest will follow."

Without waiting for a reply, she commands Clio to return to the palace. They turn back down the track, leaving the assembled slaves and their overseers in stunned silence.

Anxious priestesses run out to greet them as the Lady steps down from the chariot. A messenger has just arrived: "The land army's approaching the bridge!"

"Turn the chariot and be ready to leave again," the Lady orders Clio, and disappears into the palace. A few heartbeats later, Clio sees her at the upstairs shrine saluting Leira's clay priestess. When she reappears at the courtyard door she is carrying the sacred bronze ax on its long ash pole.

"Wait and pray," she tells the priestesses, some of

whom have begun to wail. "With this girl and her horse,
I am going to meet the invaders."

   With the four guards around the chariot, Clio drives
the Lady to the battle site.

   From the gate to the barley field,
         down the river road to the bridge,
         throng the folk from town and farms:
         crafters with hammers for bronze or stone,
         threshers with forks
         farmers with staffs;
         fishers with tridents and fishing spears.
   A mob brave in anger
         but their tools no match
         for the long handled spears,
         sharp bronze daggers,
         helmets and shields,
         of warriors marching row on row,
         down the road toward them.
   "Lady!" calls the scar-faced guard,
         when Clio stops the chariot
         at the top of the road.
         "From here you can see all there is to be seen—
         and they can see you
         in your defiance and glory."
   "But safe out of bowshot,"
         mutters the guard who limps.
   Clio reins Gray Girl
         and the guards stand close,
         two on each side.

Watching as if at sacred rites
rather than war—
"We will go where and when I say,"
murmurs the Lady to Clio,
"and the guards will obey."
Then a new cry echoes
from where the river road
meets the road to the sea—
as a black-hulled ship with a killing prow,
sides hung with warrior shields—
rows fast and straight toward their shore.
The Lady raises the sacred ax,
light glinting from its gleaming bronze,
to shout at the goddess—
"Though human souls are born to die
if you allow all our deaths today
there'll be no human hands to serve you—
the raiders bring gods of their own;
you'll live your immortal life unloved,
unpraised, unsung, unfed,
no smell of sacrifice
or wine to feast on."
As if in answer, the goddess sends
a menace of vultures, circling high,
waiting for a feast of bodies.

CHAPTER 14
THE BATTLE OF THE RAIDERS

Clio has never known
   fear so black and cold
   swelling fast to race her heart
   and stop her breath.
"Look!" cries the Lady,
   and jogging in from Gray Girl's valley
   are Petros and Ava with a troop of herders.
   Ava's arm whirrs—
   a round clay stone flies from her sling—
   so far, so true
   that a circling vulture plummets
   lifeless to the ground.
The hush as sudden as the vulture's death—
   "Closer," the Lady urges Clio,
   despite the guards' grumbling.
   They trot nearer the river

to where the Lady's voice can carry
clear to the approaching army.
"Our slingers can hit a bird on the wing—
there's a stone to the head
for each of you if you cross our bridge."
The herders in echo
whirl their slings above their heads,
the whoosh-whoosh thrumming
swelling to a roar,
a sound to strike fear
even in the heart of a warrior
for bronze helmets cover heads
but not faces
and a rock between the eyes
means death.
Gray Girl knows the whirr of a sling
but not of thirty—
Clio holds tight to her reins,
and the brave mare stands
though the four guards around them
clang spears against shields;
the folk roar defiance
and the Lady shrieks a wail of anger,
till the hairs on Clio's arms
prickle like hedgehogs.
But still the sleek ship sails in
and after their moment of fear
the raiding army jeers again,
huddling under raised shields
like a many-legged turtle

creeping step by step toward the bridge.
"Lady," says the limping guard,
    "We cannot save you
    caught in a trap between two armies—
    another heartbeat and the ship
    will be on the beach."
Clio lifts the reins—
    is stopped by a touch on her arm,
    a touch that burns
    as if the Lady has swallowed fear
    and turned it to fire.
"We'll stay," she says,
    "and defeat them all."
Then with a roar
    streaming around the chariot
    like a river around rocks
    comes an army of stinking, purple-dyed men
    waving stone hammers and small flint knives,
    great bronze cauldrons carried between them.
Marching rows of shielded warriors
    are met by the fury of purple slaves—
    slaves no more—
    each cauldron shielding three or five
    small strong men
    shoving the first warriors off the bridge
    into the river.
A clanging of battle,
    shouts and screams,
    bronze-tipped spears,
    wooden fish tridents,

round clay stones
and sharp bronze daggers.
"That is courage," says the scar-faced guard,
    "but they cannot hold.
    Lady, we will fight to the death
    to defend you
    but when the ship warriors come
    we may not be enough."
The Lady says—
    though she waves her ax as if she longs to use it—
    "I release you to fight your fiercest
    while I return to the role that is mine.
    We have offered much blood this day
    and the Great Mother still
    has the power to turn the fates.
Clio turns the mare,
    trotting fast to the palace;
    "Although I return to pray,"
    says the Lady, before she alights,
    "I feel your work is not yet done.
    In honor of this trust
    I leave the sacred ax in your care.
    Let your mare drink from a pithos
    and graze at the gate,
    ready for what the gods demand
    of her and of you.

Colti's breathing is settling but his shoulders are
lathered. Mika has to dry her hands on his mane when
she strokes him.

"Keep to a trot," she begs. "If you founder we'll never reach the Lady."

And my heart would break, she adds silently.

The colt doesn't listen. He breaks smoothly into a canter and then a gallop. But this gallop is steady and strong, not like the frantic fleeing from the purple works, and Mika is with him, body and soul. She grips with her knees, leaning forward over his neck. Her yellow shepherd's scarf catches in a tree and is lost; her long black hair mingles with the horse's mane as if they are one.

She doesn't have time to look as they pass the clifftop where she'd seen the ship. Trees pass in a blur; Colti slows on a rough bit of track and speeds again when it smooths. The purple works appear in the distance; are lost at the next bend and reappear, but the breeze is still lifting the smell away from the horse and girl. Now they're past and approaching the short road from the town to the sea. Soon she can tell the Lady the news; whatever happens after that, her job will be done.

Nearly there. Mika reins Colti back for the turn; on her left are the walls of the town; the sea just below them on the right.

They're too late.

The ship is already on the beach.

Crows caw and gulls shriek in protest. Through their cacophony a cuckoo calls its two-note whistle, over and over. Mika barely hears it. She doesn't feel the tears streaming down her face. Terror has blanked out everything except what she can see.

The last warriors are wading in; a bigger group is jogging steadily toward her. Their leader is close enough now she can see his drawn dagger and the fury on his face.

Mika tries desperately to turn Colti toward the town, but the horse slows to a shuddering stop on the edge of the beach, his shoulders foamed with sweat.

"I've killed you!" she sobs. This brave horse has run so far, so fast, he's broken his heart—and all for nothing. She'll die with him, and the town will fall because she didn't warn the Lady in time.

Colti tosses his head and trots toward the sea just as the leading raider reaches them. "Get off that horse!" he thunders, and grabs the reins.

The colt doesn't understand the danger and starts nuzzling his face.

"You can't take him!" Mika shrieks. She knows the raider's going to kill her, but she's been afraid for most of her life and she's sick of it. She's going to save Colti if she possibly can. She keeps trying to turn his head, but the man's grip is too tight.

"What have you done to my daughter?"

"Have the gods taken your wits? What would I know of your daughter? Isn't she working at home while her father raids innocent lands across the sea?"

It's as if someone else, some girl who is braver than anyone she knows, is answering through her mouth. But Mika doesn't care; she likes this girl much better than the scared one she's always been.

The raider doesn't answer. He's staring beyond

her—and then Mika hears the thunder of hooves, the rattle of wheels and the scream of rage, and she turns too.

"Let go of that horse!"

Gray Girl is galloping hard toward them. The chariot is bouncing behind her, Clio thumping on the seat. The Lady's sacred ax on its long pole stands with her crutch in its holder. Clio reaches for the ax.

Colti whinnies. The raider's hand drops from the reins. His face changes from rage to bewilderment to joy, all in the flash of a dragonfly's wing.

"Clio!" he shouts—and Mika sees her friend's face light with the same bewildered joy.

"Dada!"

As the man reaches into the chariot to hug his daughter, Mika realizes why he was running so hard. He's escaping from the pirates.

But this is not a time for hugging. The raiders are jogging toward them, armed and angry—"My crew!" Hector shouts, seeing his daughter grasp the ax again. "We took a raider's ship when they attacked us."

Petros's brother is carrying Hector's hunting bow and quiver of arrows as well as his own; he hands Hector's over and jogs on past.

"Take the message to the Lady that we're here to join the chief," Hector tells Mika, "and tell her that the raiders' ships are burning on the beach at Moklos—there'll be no attack from them."

Mika realizes that what she thought was the crying of gulls and crows was the sound of people screaming in battle. She doesn't stop to explain that the chief and his guards are somewhere on the road behind her. She turns Colti and lets him have his head up the road to the town.

"The ship is ours!" she screams as she rides. "Clio's father! And the chief and guards are following fast."

"I'll take you to the battle," says Clio to Hector.

"No! I haven't come all the way home to drag you into a war! Get your mama and Matti and flee to the hills till it's over."

"The fighting was around the bridge when I took the Lady back to the palace. It'll be faster in the chariot."

Hector hesitates. By now more of his crew have passed him on the road. "I'll ride to the town gates with you — but you're not going any closer to the battle."

He steps into the chariot, his quiver of arrows over his shoulder and his bow in his hand. Clio lets her back rest against his legs as she clucks to the mare. She wants to slow the moment, to feel this instant of joy at driving her father in the chariot he built her.

But they are driving to war. Hector is not a trained warrior, but the sailors have seen more fighting than any of the townfolk — and he is a skilled hunter. There's no joy in reunion if the raiders take the town. She urges Gray Girl to a canter. Mama and Matti are safe, she tells her father, and then fills him in on the battle.

If they all survive the day, there'll be time enough to explain about Mika, about Delia and the theft of the clay priestess; to hear how Hector had taken the raider's ship while Doulos stayed to have theirs repaired.

Hector squeezes her shoulder as they come to the top of the river road. "Flee the town now with your mama and Matti. Don't wait till the battle reaches the gates."

He jumps out. Clio takes her hands off the reins to hug him.

Gray Girl feels the reins loosen, and breaks into a trot for the familiar way home, down the river road. "Pull her back!" Hector shouts, but sudden blurring tears make Clio fumble with the dropped reins and the mare is ready to be back with her foal. They are around the first bend in the road before Clio can slow her. Hector sprints furiously behind, grabbing the chariot's side rail and swinging back on board.

They'll have to turn at the start of the path to the goat field.

But now they're around the bend, and the battle is before them and there is nothing else to see. All the raiders have made it across the bridge and are working steadily up the road toward the town, though the arrival of Hector's crew has given the defenders new energy. There are bodies on the ground and a stench of blood and filth, but it's the noise that's overwhelming: screams of rage and pain, the clang of bronze, stone, and wood. The fiercest battle seems to be around the start of the path.

There's nowhere else to turn. She'll have to go on.

"Keep low!" orders Hector, nocking an arrow to his bow.

Clio is breathless with fear but Gray Girl doesn't

hesitate. She canters down the road, ignoring the arrows flying over her head and scattering fighters out of her way as if they were gambolling goat kids. Clio barely sees them; she can concentrate on nothing but keeping the chariot steady on the road. Her father shoots arrow after arrow; the road clears ahead of them.

They thunder over the stone bridge. Gray Girl slows obediently to Clio's reins.

"Keep going!" Hector urges. "Don't let them see us turning."

They trot on around a bend to the grazed field where they can turn easily. Hector straightens, checks his bowstring, and counts the arrows left in his quiver. Six.

"Now!" he says. "Just when they think they're free of the horse, we'll burst through again. She won't trample them if she can help it, but they don't know that. When I've shot my last arrow, slow for me to jump out, then flee as fast as you can."

The scene is different looking up from the other side of the bridge. Hector's crew are pushing through to join the fight at the entrance to the goat field, where the four palace guards are surrounded by a ferocious mob of raiders. Clio sees the tallest guard fall and hears a triumphant roar from his attackers.

Hector aims an arrow carefully; he hits one raider in the leg, but can't aim into the middle of the fight for fear of hitting the guards.

Gray Girl's ears are back and her head is out. She gathers speed and bursts into a canter before the chariot is even off the bridge. As she comes around the bend at the washing rocks the canter becomes a gallop. Hector shoots another arrow, another, and another. Clio doesn't know where they land; she can see nothing but the mare and the road.

They're nearly back at the path and the whirling, roaring mass of the fight. The tall guard is up again, though his arm is covered in blood; Igor the Bronze is swinging his hammer, and Petros's brother has fought his way toward them as well. Hector's last arrow hits another raider running toward the fight—but they are still badly outnumbered.

"Slow here!" Hector hisses, stowing his bow in the crutch holder and drawing his dagger as he jumps out. For the blink of an eye, he stumbles, and in that moment, a raider races toward him, dagger swinging and his own shield up.

Clio grabs her crutch from the spear holder and swings as fast and hard as she can. She'd meant to grab the long-handled ax, but the crutch comes easily to her hand. The raider's dagger drops as the stick hits his neck and he crumples to the ground.

"Go!" shouts Hector, running toward the fight, and Gray Girl startles back into a gallop toward the roiling mass of fighters on the road. Some of the attackers turn at the thunder of hooves, terrified of being trampled. Hector fights his way through to the guards.

From the top of the hill comes the trumpet of an angry stallion.

The mare neighs back and Colti bursts into a gallop,

pounding down the river road, his smooth dark coat flecked with sweat.

The chief and the guards jog behind him, roaring as they race into the battle.

The fighters roll out of the road as the two horses meet.

"Get out of the battle!" Hector shouts at the girls.

But getting out is not that easy. The fighting is all around them, blocking the road, spilling over the track to the goat field and Gray Girl's valley. Colti trumpets again in fury. Both horses are rolling their eyes; their ears are back and tails swishing.

Colti trotting close beside Gray Girl, they push their way a little farther toward the town.

Then four raiders charge them at once. "The Lady's chariot! Take the horses!" one screams, lunging at Gray Girl's head.

The mare rears and strikes him with a fierce front hoof. He drops to the ground as Colti kicks another attacker, shattering his wooden shield and throwing him backwards. He spins and kicks again as a third raider reaches for Mika's foot to drag her off. The man lands on the ground, doubling up in pain as the fourth man grabs the chariot traces.

This time Clio grabs the sacred ax when she means to. The pole is long, much longer than her crutch. She swings it hard. At the same moment Gray Girl turns her head to bite the attacker.

Blood gushes. For a terrible, terrible heartbeat, Clio thinks she's hit her beloved mare.

The raider screams, clutching his bloodied hand against his chest.

As if by magic, the road clears in front of the girls and their horses. The fighting slows around them, attackers and defenders caught by the scene.

The raiders have already lost twelve men against this motley band of townfolk, herders, and slaves; now the sailors are pushing them back toward the river, the palace guards have regained their ground, and sixteen more trained warriors are pouring onto the field. But it's seeing four of his strongest fighters on the ground around two girls and their horses that decides the captain on what he must do.

He steps forward toward the chief, holding his spear upside down to call for a truce.

CHAPTER 15
CHOOSING THE FUTURE

Usually in the spring festival, once the sacrifices have been accepted and the Lady has read the oracle for the coming season, she doesn't make any more pronouncements. It is simply time to rejoice and party.

This isn't a usual spring festival. Two farmers, a carpenter, two purple workers, and Mika's brother Dymos lie dead. They will be honored the next day, but the families wail now. Except Mika. She doesn't know what she feels.

And Dada is home. Matti has been riding on his shoulders or clinging to his leg and is determined never to let go of him again. He's heard Mika's story and welcomed her. "If the colt accepts you, you are part of our family," he declares. He can't find words to say just how proud he is of Clio, but his glowing face and the hand on her shoulder say more than words.

It's hard to believe it's still the same day they'd

gathered in the court to see the Lady accept the clay priestess and return Delia to life.

As the sacred bonfires welcome back the townfolk who fled to the hills, Clio feels that the whole festival could be simply to celebrate the reunion of all her family and friends. The meat is roasted and shared, the feast cups are used and smashed, the events of the day are worked into family sagas.

Then the guards bang spears on shields again, stopping hearts for a beat or three. "The Lady will speak," bellows the chief, and she mounts the stage in the court.

"In this day of the Great Mother's full moon to welcome the spring, we have seen great changes. Changes that will bring new life for all who choose it.

"We have made peace with the raiders. We will return their army to where they have settled; they have sworn a great oath before their god and ours that they will not attack again but will learn to live and trade as good neighbors in peace.

"The slaves of the purple works are slaves no more and will be welcomed into the town as any other craft-folk.

"Our goddess has shown us that perfection lies not only in the body but in the soul; that courage is no less when walked with a crutch, and a mind that is open to change is worth more than gold."

No need for the crutch with arms linked tight,
   Clio dances with old friends and new,

warm with the glow of the Lady's words—
"The goddess had her reasons
for keeping you from the ballot—
though it's not easy for humans to understand
the many faces of perfect."
So she dances and sings
and so does Mika,
the cuckoo girl welcomed in,
free to work with herders and horses;
with Delia who can choose
to continue as potter
or serve in the temple living and strong;
Petros who will always love
his herders' life
but has learned to lead as well;
while Clio herself can choose the clay
or the horses—or both—
for the Lady also said,
"You are the daughter and granddaughter
of master potters—
their gifts will show—
but you have another talent as well—
I ask that you would train
both horses and priestesses
for the taste of freedom
you have given me this day."
And like sun bursting through clouds
Clio sees
that freedom is part of her
just as much as her wounded leg;

whatever path she follows
or how life will be
she'll choose with her heart
and that path
will be her own.

AUTHOR'S NOTE

Cuckoo's Flight takes place in the same world as *Dragonfly Song* and *Swallow's Dance*, based on the Minoan civilization of Crete about four thousand years ago. It was a sophisticated and artistic culture whose ships traded as far away as Cyprus and Egypt, but it was eventually overtaken by the Mycenaeans from mainland Greece, probably by a mixture of warfare and assimilation.

Although Crete had indigenous horses, the Minoans don't seem to have used them as much as many other Bronze Age societies. However, in a tiny museum in Archanes in Crete, I saw a Minoan clay figurine of a woman riding a horse. I started wondering about her...

At the same time, my sister Katharine was planning a horseback trip through Mongolia. Her travels reignited my dreams of the joy and freedom of riding, even though an accident has left me unable to continue to do so. Partway through the first draft I realized that my protagonist Clio was disabled and, like me, could no longer ride.

The later drafts of this book were written during the COVID-19 pandemic and lockdown. In many ways we returned to an earlier time: our family became a multi-generational household, afraid of an uncertain future and a disease that appeared to have no cure. All these factors made *Cuckoo's Flight* a slightly different book than it would have been otherwise. I've finished the book without seeing the end of the pandemic but, in life as in fiction, I remain hopeful of the future.

ACKNOWLEDGMENTS

The last eight months of writing this book have made me more grateful than ever for my family's love and support, but my daughter-in-law Georgia deserves a special thanks. In the chaos of a home with shared office space and two toddlers, she took over all the cooking and ensured that there was always time for me to write.

Thanks to my editors and publishers at both Allen & Unwin and Pajama Press for their encouragement and faith in this book, even when I was eight months late on my deadline: Jodie Webster and Kate Whitfield; Gail Winskill and Erin Alladin. Also to Josh Durham for another glorious cover and Sarfaraaz Alladin for his meticulous and charming maps—I really appreciate them.

I'd also like to extend thanks to the Australia Council for the Arts again for the grant to research *Swallow's Dance* in Crete, which also brought this story to life for me; to Bernadette Kelly for answering horsemanship questions; and to Hugh Dolan for the Bronze Age battle advice, especially the sound of massed slings.

ABOUT THE AUTHOR

Wendy Orr was born in Canada, and grew up in France, Canada, and the USA. After high school, she studied occupational therapy in England, married an Australian farmer, and moved to Australia. They had a son and a daughter, and now live on five acres of bush near the sea. Her books have won awards in Australia and around the world, and have been translated into twenty-seven languages.

Although Wendy first learned to read and write in French, her family spoke English at home. She clearly remembers the excitement of reading a story in her own language for the first time. She immediately started writing stories, and hasn't stopped since.

Wendy has had many highlights in her writing career, including being a finalist for the TD Canadian Children's Literature Award and walking a red carpet with Jodie Foster, but believes that nothing compares to the thrill of the first vision of a new book.